"Does it amuse you, Ros, to play hard to get?"

"I don't know what you mean, Keel," Ros replied innocently. "I'm here to help Milly act as hostess. That's what I'm being paid for, after all."

"But you're not paid to devote all of your time to the crowd gathered around her."

"A hostess has to dance with all the guests."

"And I'm a guest. So I'm entitled to an equal share of your attention," Keel responded smoothly as he captured her for a dance. "So at least try to pretend you're enjoying yourself, if only to please Milly."

"I am enjoying myself. I'm enjoying the music," Ros snapped as Keel tightened his embrace.

"Good, because I'll have the last waltz as well."

Sue Peters grew up in the idyllic countryside of
Warwickshire, England, and began writing romance
novels quite by chance. "Have a go," her mother
suggested when a national writing contest sponsored
by Mills & Boon appeared in the local newspaper.
Sue's entry placed second, and a career was born.
After completing her first romance novel, she missed
the characters so much she started another and
another.... Now she's as addicted to writing as she is
to gardening, which she often does as she's
formulating new plots.

Books by Sue Peters

HARLEQUIN ROMANCE
1975—CLOUDED WATERS
2030—ONE SPECIAL ROSE
2104—PORTRAIT OF PARADISE
2156—LURE OF THE FALCON
2204—ENTRANCE TO THE HARBOUR
2351—SHADOW OF AN EAGLE
2368—CLAWS OF A WILDCAT
2410—MARRIAGE IN HASTE
2423—TUG OF WAR
2471—DANGEROUS RAPTURE
2501—MAN OF TEAK
2583—LIGHTNING STRIKES TWICE
2812—NEVER TOUCH A TIGER
2892—ENTRANCE TO EDEN

Don't miss any of our special offers. Write to us at the
following address for information on our newest releases.

Harlequin Reader Service
901 Fuhrmann Blvd., P.O. Box 1397, Buffalo, NY 14240
Canadian address: P.O. Box 603,
Fort Erie, Ont. L2A 5X3

Capture a
Nightingale
Sue Peters

Harlequin Books

TORONTO • NEW YORK • LONDON
AMSTERDAM • PARIS • SYDNEY • HAMBURG
STOCKHOLM • ATHENS • TOKYO • MILAN

Original hardcover edition published in 1987
by Mills & Boon Limited

ISBN 0-373-02915-2

Harlequin Romance first edition June 1988

Printed in U.S.A.

CHAPTER ONE

'ISN'T it typical of Lyn? She's left out the one thing which could be of any help.' Ros poked exasperated fingers into the envelope, and frowned when it remained obdurately empty.

'She's sent you an airline ticket. Where's it to?' With the freedom of friendship, Sally reached out for the paperwork lying beside her flatmate's breakfast plate, and squeaked excitedly. 'It's to Majorca! And it's dated the day after tomorrow. Lucky you! Sunshine and sandy beaches. What's it all in aid of, Ros? I didn't know Lyn could afford to give away free airline tickets.'

'If you'll shut up for a minute, I'll read you her letter.'

Sally subsided, and Ros straightened out her friend's hastily penned note and read, 'Ros, help! I've been offered a part in the London production *Friendly Gathering*. Imagine, turning professional after all this time with the Amateur Operatic Society. It's my big break. I can't afford to turn it down.'

'She'll be mad if she does.'

'Lyn's very sane,' Ros responded drily. 'It's me who must be mad, to put up with her pushing me around. Listen.'

She continued to read, still trying to take in the

contents of the letter herself. Lyn wrote, 'I was due to go to Majorca to help out my godmother for a couple of weeks. She's Mildred Fisher, the painter.'

'Isn't she the one who signs her paintings with a capital M, with a fish swimming through it?' Sally asked. 'She's supposed to be flavour of the month in the painting world, and fabulously rich.'

'I believe so. I'm not much into painting myself. I've seen her picture in the papers, but I don't know what her work's like. According to this,' Ros tapped the letter, 'she's holding an exhibition of her work, and the world's flocking to Majorca to view.'

'That'll be great. You'll have a super time.'

'You haven't heard the rest of it yet. The crunch is still to come. Lyn's concerned about her godmother. She says Mildred Fisher's terribly other-worldly, and sees nothing except her paintings. She fills her house with guests she hardly knows, and gets a lot of hangers-on who're out for all they can get.'

Rapidly Ros scanned the rest of the hastily written page, which begged, 'I know it's an awful cheek, but will you go over to Majorca and act as a sort of girl Friday, in my place? Now the musical's finished, you'll be at a loose end for a bit.'

'You'll go, of course?' Sally interrupted. 'You can't turn down a fortnight in the Mediterranean.'

'I haven't got much option. By now, Lyn's half-way to London to join the new cast. She made sure I didn't get a chance to refuse.'

'Then start packing. You've got nothing to lose.' Sally stopped awkwardly.

'You're right. I've got nothing to lose.'

In spite of herself, Ros could not keep a note of bitterness from her voice. Now the musical was finished, so was the occupation that had filled the blank hours since her firm had folded, and her job as PA to its managing director had gone with it.

And she had lost Lomas Deering.

During the last few months, the amateur company had played to packed houses, and during their spare time she and the leading man had been inseparable. Except, that is, at night, when Ros had been adamant that they parted company, and each had returned to their own flat.

She had answered Lomas's urgent protests, 'I love you, Ros,' with a firm, 'And I love you. After we're married . . .'

His reaction had left Ros shocked and dismayed.

'Who said anything about marriage? We're artists, Ros. Artists have got to be free spirits. They can't be tied by such mundane things as marriage.'

Ros's lips twisted cynically at the memory.

Artists? They were all amateurs. She was an out-of-work secretary and Lomas was an accountant during the day. This time, he had got his sums wrong; Ros had unhesitatingly slapped down his aspiration to become her lover with no strings attached.

It was a new slant to the age-old philosophy of, take what you want and run. She would never trust any man again, she vowed. Somehow she had managed to get through the final night of the musical. She had responded to Lomas's airy farewell, 'See you around,' with a silent, 'Not if I can help it,' and taken herself back to the flat she shared with

Sally, grateful for the fact that, although she had lost Lomas, she had retained her self-respect.

It did nothing to help the rawness inside her, which smarted like an open wound. A fortnight in Majorca would not only provide her with much needed paid work, it would also stop her from brooding.

'If only Lyn had remembered to send the photograph she promised with her letter,' she grumbled. 'It wouldn't matter if she'd given me her godmother's address on Majorca, but all I know is that Mildred Fisher lives at the Casa Mimosa, somewhere on the island.'

'Finding a famous artist shouldn't prove difficult.'

'It wouldn't be, normally, but apparently she's only just bought the place and moved in, and she's combining a house-warming and the exhibition at the same time. Places like the embassy, who would know where she's located, might not have got the message yet.'

'How did Lyn expect you to find the place if she didn't give you the address?'

'An old family friend of the Fishers is travelling on the same plane. Lyn's arranged with him to take me along. She says,' Ros referred again to the letter, 'I'm enclosing his photograph so that you'll recognise him, and I've sent him a press cutting of our musical so that he'll know who you are. His name's Keel Hennessy.'

'Sounds interesting.' Sally grinned.

'Not to me. I'm through with men. Anyway, Lyn says he's an old friend of the family, so the accent will be on the world "old". From the Press photographs

I've seen of her, Mildred Fisher must be sixty if she's a day, so her friends are bound to be of the same generation.'

Ros walked into the departure lounge at the airport two days later, and wondered which of her fellow passengers was Keel Hennessy.

She surveyed the assembled male travellers from under the curiously dark lashes that made such an effective frame for her deep violet eyes. Curious because the sooty lashes contrasted so sharply with her spun gold hair, that for the purposes of her journey she had restrained in a wide comb-slide at the nape of her neck, drawing it demurely round the delicately boned oval of her face, and allowing it to fall in a shining rope across her shoulders.

The looks she received in return were less circumspect. Women's eyes openly envied her slender figure, shown off to perfection by the lightweight silver-grey suit and the cashmere sweater of the same soft violet as her eyes, highlighted by a gold rope necklace that reflected the bright glints from her hair.

The eyes of the men were . . .

Ros dismissed them. She was accustomed to being stared at, and knew without vanity that her own refined beauty would always command attention wherever she went. Her own problem was of more immediate importance. Names gave no clue to a person's identity, she discovered ruefully.

Keel Hennessy. She said it over softly to herself. His surname sounded faintly Irish. Or was it Scottish? Keel smacked vaguely of the sea. Ros smiled inwardly. If his name was any guide, she should be looking for an elderly sailor in a kilt, and none of the assembled company fitted that description.

Their age range fitted, however. They consisted mostly of elderly holidaymakers intent on seeking an early suntan, with only a scattering of younger, jet-set business types among them, doubtless bound for Paris, where the passengers for Majorca had to change planes, all the direct flights having apparently been fully booked.

Ros turned her attention to the holidaymakers as they boarded the plane. Any one of them could fit the description of 'old friend of the family'. One in particular looked the part, with a luxuriant growth of beard sprouting untidily round his face. Definitely an arty type, and a likely friend of Mildred Fisher.

Ros smiled sweetly at him and enquired, 'Are you Mr Hennessy? Mr Keel Hennessy?'

'No, dearie.' The beard split in a grin. 'But I'm willing to impersonate him, if it means going along with you.'

Ros stammered, 'I'm sorry,' and retreated in haste, deciding to ask the stewardess as they disembarked rather than repeat the experiment. Keel Hennessy must be on the passenger list, and the stewardess would be able to identify him.

He could be joining the island flight in Paris, of course. Ros wished that Lyn had been more precise in her letter, and then she thrust all conjecture aside as the plane climbed bumpily through the cloud mass, and emerged into a brilliant sunlit world that made the early April cold below seem unreal.

Grasping at the travellers' joy of problems left behind, and those to come still far away, she tackled the piping hot meal put before her by the stewardess and, that done, she must have dozed, because she opened her eyes to see the illuminated warning sign flashing on above her head. Obediently she fastened her seatbelt, and nerved herself for another attempt to find Keel Hennessy.

The discovery that he was not after all on the Paris flight cheered her somewhat, and she rescued her luggage and made her way through the terminal building to her next departure point in a more hopeful frame of mind. The waiting areas seemed to be unusually quiet. There were less people than Ros remembered from previous visits, and those who were there stood about in uncertain looking groups. All except one man.

He stood alone.

He would have stood alone in any crowd, Ros thought. He was the sort of man you would be conscious of at a hundred yards distance, in total darkness, and he was impossible to ignore. His personality was so strong that it projected like a tangible force across the airport lounge, sending out feelers like invisible antennae to touch and discover her reaction to him.

His tall, athletic frame lifted him head and shoulders above the rest of the crowd, and his outstanding good looks would mark him out in any gathering. He was only too well aware of them himself, Ros decided critically. She felt her skin prickle as she met his cool scrutiny.

If he expected her to respond, he was due to be disappointed. Physical beauty, including her own, was an accident of nature, and Ros regarded pride as only being justified by personal achievement.

His piercing stare began to get on her nerves, and abruptly she turned her back, shutting it off. It was a move she had used countless times before to warn off unwelcome attention, and usually it succeeded, but this time the looker seemed impervious to her hint.

Even with her back turned towards him, Ros could still feel his eyes watching her, and she flashed her own urgently round the other passengers, wishing her escort would come and declare himself. If he did not do so soon, she would have a call sent out on the loudhailer system for him. The lone stranger did not qualify. He was about twenty-five years too young.

'Attention . . .'

Ros put down her suitcase and listened as the announcement warned her that the flight to Majorca was unlikely to take off that day. The disembodied voice regretted any inconvenience to passengers, but a lightning strike by air traffic controllers had grounded all aircraft until further notice.

Ros groaned out loud. 'What now?'

'Come with me,' a voice commanded. A hand grasped her arm, and Ros spun sharply to confront its owner.

It was the man who had stood alone. He picked up her suitcase and began to hustle her towards the glass swing doors.

'Just a minute.' Ros twisted her arm free from his grasp.

'We haven't got a minute if we're to catch . . .'

'I'm not going to catch anything, to go anywhere, with you.'

Did he imagine she was so naïve that she would allow herself to be picked up by a stranger, and dragged off without a word of protest? He was supremely sure of himself, and Ros's hackles rose to combat his arrogance.

He had a devil-may-care tilt to his head, and a glint in the curious clear amber of his eyes that told her he was a law unto himself, and conceded no one the right to cross his path; not even air traffic controllers. Still less herself.

He fixed his strange eyes on Ros with a fierce intensity that made her blink.

'You're Ros Morland, on your way to the Casa Mimosa?'

Ros's head jerked up. Surely this could not be Keel Hennessy? An old friend of Mildred Fisher's family? Old? He could not be more than thirty-three or four, and his lean figure, in perfect trim, questioned even that.

'Yes, I'm Ros Morland. But who . . .'

'I'm Keel Hennessy. Keel to you. Surely my photograph isn't so awful that you can't recognise me? I knew you immediately. But in case you're nervous of going with a stranger, here's the Press cutting Lyn sent to me. Now are you satisfied?'

He reached into the pocket of his perfectly tailored jacket and flicked a neatly folded newspaper cutting under her nose.

Ros nodded dumbly. So much for her preconceived notion of what her escort's age would be. She had been so sure he would be of the artist's own generation, and now she had been proved wrong by this stranger, to whom she had just administered an unmistakable snub.

Mentally blacking Lyn for her absent-mindedness, she began stiffly, 'I don't . . .' when Keel cut her short.

'Go with strangers? No nice girl does,' he mocked.

Ros's colour rose at his taunt. 'If you'd listen, I was going to say I don't have your advantage. Lyn forgot to include your photograph in the letter she sent to me.'

'That figures, with Lyn. She'd forget her head if it was loose, like all her sex.'

'You've got a low opinion of women.'

'Prove me wrong,' he gibed, but before Ros could open her mouth to retort he recaptured her arm in a hold that she knew vexedly she would find it impossible to break free from, this time, and growled,

'Do you want to reach the Casa Mimosa today, or not?'

'Of course I do, but . . .'

'Then stop arguing, and come with me.'

His grip left her with no option, and the speed with which he pulled her along left Ros with no breath to argue. He hurried her through the swing doors and into a waiting cab with a brusque, 'Hop in,' giving her a thrust that made sure she obeyed him.

She hoped fervently that Lyn had known what she was doing when she had put her in charge of this forceful creature. He was taking charge with a surety and completeness that she found unnerving. He slammed the door on them as the driver slung Ros's case on top of another, expensive-looking holdall with the initials KH emblazoned across one corner.

Keel must have learned about the stoppage at the airport, and had his plans already formulated when he came into the terminal building in search of her. He was a fast mover, Ros conceded, and wondered with a slight shiver in exactly which context she meant.

Out loud, she demanded, 'Where are we going?'

'The Hotel Cher.'

With an economy of words Keel used his instruction to the driver as her answer, and sat back in his seat as the cab swung into the traffic. Ros sat bolt upright, and stared at him, aghast.

'I can't possibly stay at the Cher. At least, not unless the airline's prepared to pay.'

It was one of the premier hotels in the city, and must charge the earth.

'We're not staying there. We're only leaving our luggage.'

'I can't leave my luggage behind, either. I'll only have what I stand up in if I do.'

'The things you can't do seem to be legion. I'll give you another one to add to your list. You can't take your luggage along, because the route we're taking to the Casa Mimosa doesn't allow for heavy suitcases. I've arranged for them to follow us later. Milly will lend you a nightie. You're about her build.'

His eyes assessed Ros's build with cool effrontery, and her lips tightened. How much later? And which route did he mean? She opened her mouth to fire her questions at him, just as the taxi driver stood on his brakes.

As the imposing facade of the Cher loomed through her side window, Ros, unable to help herself, slid to the front of her seat and grabbed for an anchor to stop herself from sliding right off it and on to the floor.

The anchor her clutching fingers found was Keel Hennessy.

She let go of his jacket sleeve as it if was hot, and wriggled back into her seat as the cab driver leapt out of his own, and disappeared into the hotel with the luggage.

Keel remained seated calmly beside her.

'You don't have to stay with me. I shan't decamp, if that's what you're worried about,' Ros told him abruptly, surprised that he did not follow the taxi driver into the hotel to make sure they were prepared to take the luggage. 'I'm as anxious to reach Majorca as you are.'

'It wouldn't worry me in the least if you did,' her companion assured her, and his well-cut lips tilted at the look she shot him. 'It might worry Milly, though,' he added, and raised his voice as the cab driver returned. 'The Gare du Nord now, Pierre, and fast,' he instructed.

'Did you have to?' Ros groaned as the cab driver proceeded to carry out his orders with nerve shattering efficiency.

Horns blared and tyres screeched, and they sped through the city streets rocking round corners at a terrifying angle on what Ros felt convinced must be two wheels. After the second such corner she became aware of a steel-strong arm holding her back in her seat.

She looked round, startled. The feel of Keel's arm was even more unnerving than the cab man's suicidal driving, although she blamed the latter for her suddenly wobbly legs when the taxi jerked to a halt.

Her companion shot through the door, pulling her along with him. Coins changed hands, and Keel took Ros by the arm and began to run.

'Don't go so fast,' she gasped. 'I'm getting a stitch.'

For answer he shifted his arm to her waist and lifted her along with him without slackening speed, through the ticket barrier, across the platform, towards the sleek express which was poised on the point of departure.

He shouted. A door opened in front of them and Ros felt her feet leave the ground as Keel picked her up bodily and thrust her inside the train, and joined her himself with a mighty leap just as the steel monster began to move.

'Made it,' he said calmly, and grinned.

Perfect teeth glinted in his deeply tanned face, but the grin held no triumph, only a jaunty confidence that its owner could take on even a French express train, and win.

Ros wondered suddenly if anyone had ever had the temerity to take on Keel Hennessy. And, if so, what had been the result?

Silly question, her intuition scolded. The result would be a foregone conclusion.

'You can get your breath back now,' he said, and settled Ros into a comfortable window seat with an old world courtesy that was at variance with the cavalier way in which he had heaved her on to the train.

Ros sat back limply, and studied him. He possessed unusually high cheekbones which, if it had not been for his cultured and very English voice, would have made her suspect American Indian ancestry. His shock of hair was nut brown and wavy, and cropped uncompromisingly close above his high forehead, and his lips . . . Ros's attention sharpened on his lips. They were firm, and well cut, but the lower lip had a slight sensual fullness that hinted at unsuspected depths behind his authoriatative exterior.

A thought strayed across her mind, tantalising her. What would it be like to test those depths?

'Coffee?' the subject of her thoughts enquired, and hastily Ros reined in her straying thoughts.

'Thank you,' she mumbled.

What had come over her? She had kissed enough handsome men on the lips in the course of her amateur stage work to remain impervious to one more pair.

She had remained impervious, until Lomas. But that was over, and she did not intend to repeat her mistake. She lowered her lashes under his quizzical stare, and accepted her coffee from the hovering steward.

Refusing milk, she sipped gratefully, thankful for the liquid darkness to combat the unsteadiness that seemed to have travelled from her knees to her hands, making the cup clink sharply against the saucer.

She spoke hurriedly, hoping Keel had not noticed the sign of her nervousness.

'Do you mind telling me where we're heading for?'

'Le Havre.'

'Le Havre? she echoed. 'What's the point of going to the coast? We need to get another airport: Nantes, or Bordeaux.'

'The strike's nationwide. All the French airports will be at a standstill until it's over. It's pointless to attempt to sit it out,' he insisted as Ros opened her mouth to argue. 'It could take days before it's settled. I know of a better way, by boat.'

He would. Ros frowned. If they were going the rest of the way by boat, why could they not bring their luggage along with them?

'Why can't . . .' she began abruptly, then stopped, nonplussed. Keel leaned back in his seat, and closed his eyes. Was he dozing? Or had he closed his lids against her, anticipating her question and, for reasons best known to himself, being unwilling to answer it?

Ros suspected the latter, and felt a prick of uneasiness. She did not doubt Keel was who he said he was. How else would he have the press cutting in his pocket, and speak so easily of Lyn and Milly? And, too, the initials on his suitcase fitted. But it was one thing to accept a strange escort on a public conveyance such as an aircraft, and quite another to take off across France on a wild-goose chase alone with that same stranger.

How well did Lyn really know him? The fact that he was a friend of her godmother did not make him trustworthy company under the circumstances. In retrospect, his haste to drag her away from the airport was suspicious.

Another couple came to sit beside them, and their presence constrained Ros's impulse to shake her companion awake and demand that he be more specific about the rest of their journey.

Why had she allowed herself to be rushed into this cross-country trek, bereft of everything except her handbag and the clothes she stood up in, instead of doing the sensible thing and sitting out the strike in Paris? It would probably be over in twenty-four hours.

Had her companion thought the same, and deliberately rushed her off with him before she had had time to think? Twenty-four hours' delay in reaching the Casa Mimosa would not have made all that much difference, so what was his hurry?

Another thought occurred to Ros to add to her unease. If she herself had been plain, and middle-aged, would her escort have bothered to rush her off in a manner which, she realised with a frown, put her very much at his mercy?

Beauty could be a snare; Ros had early learned to step warily round its noose. If Keel hoped to pull it tight, he would find himself with a captive possessed of lots of fight, she promised herself grimly. If she needed any further lesson on that score, Lomas had provided it. After him, she trusted no man.

The train slowed and swung into a station, and the noise and bustle of the platform put an end to Ros's thoughts. She glanced across at Keel, and felt a tremor run through her. His eyes were wide open, and watching her. Confirming her suspicion that he had been foxing all along.

How long had he been watching her? Ros could not tell. While she had been studying his face, thinking he slept, had he all the time been studying her from under lowered lids, fully aware of her scrutiny? And—her cheeks warmed—did he imagine her interest in him to be a personal one?

Keel stood up. 'Time to go,' he said, and pushed open the carriage door. He swung down on to the platform and reached up a hand to help Ros to disembark, taking her fingers in a strong, sure grip, the better to steer her through the milling crowds on the platform.

His closeness was disconcerting. There was a curious magnetism about him that did not rely upon his distinguished looks, and Ros felt the pull of it uncomfortably strong, heightened by the feel of the whipcord hardness of his arm against her own. She wished she had the excuse of her suitcase to occupy her hand and arm, and draw her away from him to a safer distance. Which reminded her.

'Why can't we . . .' she began.

'Ask me later, when we're on board,' he cut her short. 'Let's get through this scrum first.'

He signalled to a waiting cab, and Ros's desire to ask questions vanished for the time being. The driver repeated the performance of his Parisian counterpart. Were all French taxi drivers devoid of nerves? Ten shattered minutes later the taxi stopped on a concrete hard, and Ros took stock of her surroundings while Keel paid off the driver.

They were at the entrance to a small harbour, and her eyes searched for the expected boat. There were private yachts aplenty, lined up neatly at their moorings, but there was nothing approaching the passenger-carrying ferry she expected to see. She turned up the collar of her suit jacket, and hoped they would not have long to wait.

A cutting wind sliced across the uneasy waters, raising choppy waves that made Ros thankful they would be travelling on a large vessel. The private yachts moored nearby tossed like so many corks on the swell, and made her distinctly un-nautical stomach feel queasy just to look at them.

She shivered, and cast a longing look at the booking office at the end of a long landing stage, where presumably the boat they had come to catch would dock. She hoped they would be able to wait inside it, out of the wind, until the boat came.

Keel took her arm and said, 'Let's go somewhere warmer,' but instead of steering her towards the booking office he guided her the other way along the line of moored vessels.

A gangplank protruded from one side of the largest sea-going yacht, with the name *Sea Spray* painted on its side. Ros noticed the wheeled end of a small railed walkway rolling busily backwards and forwards across the hard in time to the uneasy tossing of the vessel. None of the other yachts had their gangplanks out, so probably it was put ready for someone to come down it.

Or to go up.

Realisation dawned upon Ros seconds before Keel said,

'You'll soon be in the warm now. Up you go.'

This was worse than she had anticipated. It was a private yacht. If she went on board, she would be completely on her own with Keel, and cut off from any other human contact. Ros baulked.

'I thought you said we'd be going by boat.'

'This is a boat.'

'I can see that.' Nerves sharpened her voice. 'But . . .'

'Hi, Keel!'

A heavily duffle-coated figure appeared on deck and hailed them. 'You made good time,' he said. 'You'll be able to use the tide.' He nodded in a friendly fashion to Ros, and Keel said, 'Ros, this is Tim.'

Ros nodded, but her face was too stiff with cold to smile. Tim said, 'You're not dressed for standing about in this wind. Best go below and thaw out. Ella's stowing away some groceries in the gallery.'

Ella. Another girl was on board. Ros scorned herself for the relief that flooded through her as she turned up the gangplank. It was of paramount importance to get warm if she was not to arrive on Majorca suffering from pneumonia, and she forced her frozen feet up to the deck as another duffle-coated figure surfaced from below, a shorter, slighter figure this time, but equally well wrapped up against the cold.

'I saw you coming,' Ella greeted her cheerfully, 'so I brewed up. You'll find the teapot in the galley.'

Ros could have hugged her. 'A hot cup of tea sounds bliss.'

'There's a tot in the cupboard to mix with it,' Ella grinned. 'It'll ward off the effects of the cold. Go below while Tim and I help Keel to cast off. I didn't have time to put out the cups. You'll find them in the cupboard with the rum.'

'Give a hand here, Ella,' Tim called, and the other girl hurried off.

Ros smiled as she went below. Ella seemed nice. She looked forward to getting acquainted, but there was no point in offering her help now. She had no knowledge of boats, and would only be in the way.

She felt her way cautiously down the companionway into the galley, grateful for the warmth that cocooned her as she searched out four cups and saucers ready for when the others came down.

The homely brown crock teapot was large and heavy, and there was a fresh carton of milk on the table. Ros hesitated as she looked at the rum. Should she use it, or not? The last thing she wanted was to collect a streaming cold, and Ella's advice to lace her tea was sensible.

How much rum should she use? So far as Ros was concerned, it was unexplored liquid territory. It might taste just as awful as whisky, which she hated.

She uncapped the bottle and sniffed cautiously. It smelled nicer than whisky. A sudden fit of shivering decided her. Her hand shook with the shivers, and she spilled out more rum than she intended, but the steam from the cup smelled pleasant, and a wary sip sent warmth seeping right through her.

Unidentifiable sounds percolated downwards from the deck above her head, which she assumed to be connected with the casting off. A loud slap, as of a hard rope hitting the deck, and a mechanical-sounding rattle, told of busy activity. An engine sprang into life, and the boat began to vibrate.

Ros wondered how long it would take them to reach Majorca by sea. She took another sip of her tea, and felt the warmth begin to relax her frozen muscles. She reached over and milked the rest of the cups in readiness for when the others came down.

She hoped Ella would come first, before the men. She wanted to talk to Ella; the other girl would be easier to question than Keel, and Ros's mind teemed with questions. To her chagrin she discovered they mostly centred round Keel. The fact that he had taken such complete control of her did nothing for her peace of mind.

There were a lot of gaps which she would like to fill in before she reached the Casa Mimosa. Perhaps Tim and Ella were to be among the guests? She hoped so. She had taken an instant liking to them both, which was more than she could say about her escort. His high-handed manner grated on her independent spirit, and rubbed at nerves that still felt raw from Lomas.

The minutes stretched, and sounds from overhead ceased; all, that was, except the steady purr of the engine. The motion of the yacht underwent a subtle change, and Ros judged that they were now clear of the harbour, and heading out into the open sea.

She sent up a silent prayer that her stomach would behave itself. She was not a good sailor, and an apprehensive glance through the porthole revealed heaving waters that, if she looked at them for long, would tempt her stomach to follow suit.

Hurriedly, Ros withdrew her gaze. The last thing

she wanted was to suffer the humiliation of being seasick in front of Keel. A breath of fresh air might avert disaster, she decided. The others were still on deck. They must be impervious to the cold, but presumably would welcome a cup of tea.

She finished her own, and after a quick rummage discovered a tin tray, which she loaded with three cups and the teapot, adding the bottle of rum before cautiously making her way up the companionway.

A blast of icy air turned her hurriedly into the shelter of the wheelhouse, where Keel stood with one had resting lightly on the wheel, swaying easily to the motion of the boat.

He was alone.

He turned as Ros came in, and reached across to relieve her of the heavy tray.

'I thought you'd like a cup of tea,' she said. Now she was confronting him, and could ask her questions, she felt curiously tongue-tied; another more urgent question needed to be answered right away.

Where were Ella and Tim?

'Thoughtful of you,' Keel commented, 'but why three cups? Are you one of those people who always caters for absent friends?'

'They're for Ella and Tim, of course. Where are they?'

'In the harbour bistro, thawing out, if they've got any sense.'

'You mean, they're not with us?'

Ridiculously, Ros felt as if her mouth had dropped open. Too late it dawned upon her that to help someone to cast off must mean going ashore to free mooring ropes from bollards.

'Does it bother you?' Keel mocked.

It bothered Ros more than she was prepared to admit. Keel was devastatingly attractive, and knew it. Just as she knew the force of her own beauty, and the inflammatory effect if could have upon men. Together they added up to potentially explosive ingredients, but if Keel tried to stir the mixture, she promised she would make it blow up in his face.

To avoid answering him she bent to pour out a cup of tea, and handed it to him, leaving him to add rum himself if he wanted it.

'Thanks. What about yours?'

'I've had mine.'

'Have another?'

'Not now.'

Her stomach began to churn uncomfortably, with nerves, and the motion of the yacht. It distracted her mind from the things she wanted to ask Keel, and suddenly it became urgent to return below before he could begin to suspect how she felt.

'If you've finished your tea, I'll go and wash up,' she said, and took his empty cup.

'Toss a meal together while you're about it. Ella put some food in the galley.'

He did not say, 'Will you?' He took it for granted that she would obey what was tantamount to an order from the master of the vessel to a galley hand. Ros bridled. Presumably Keel knew why she was going to the Casa Mimosa, and regarded her in the light of one of its staff, accepting it as his right to give her orders.

Her hackles rose at his arrogance, but just as she was about to send back a swingeing retort the vessel slipped from the crest of a huge wave into an equally deep trough, immediately to tilt its bow upwards again to rise to the next comber.

Ros gulped and grabbed the tray, and fled below, but not before she caught the glint of laughter in the eyes of the man at the wheel, eyes that saw her discomfiture, and derided it.

Had he deliberately mentioned food so as to make it worse? Annoyed, Ros would not have put it past him. The possibility stung her pride and, not to be outdone, she took out some food to place on the galley table. Ella had catered for good appetites with a couple of crusty pastry-covered pies, still hot, probably homemade takeaways from the harbour bistro. These Ros slid into the oven to keep hot, and as she did so a rich and succulent aroma rose from their meaty interiors.

It was the last straw.

She gagged, and a wave of faintness passed over her. He legs began to buckle, and hurriedly she subsided on to a chair, groaning aloud as she ducked her head below her knees.

'That's all I need, a seasick female,' Keel's voice said disgustedly from the spinning world above her head. She felt a hard arm come round her back, and another under her knees, lifting her up.

She felt past caring what Keel needed. Her own needs occupied her mind to the exclusion of everything else, and the most urgent was . . .

When it was over Keel washed her face and dried it with a briskly wielded towel before lifting Ros on to a bunk, and cocooning her shivering body in the blessed warmth of a blanket, with the observation, 'You'll sleep now.'

Was that an order, too?

Her eyelids wanted to obey it. They felt too heavy to lift themselves. Ros felt the blanket being tucked tightly round her, holding her securely in the bunk against the uneasy tossing of the vessel, while an amused voice percolated her dazed mind, commenting with destructive honesty,

'Your face is green enough for you to impersonate Kermit without wearing make-up.'

Ros turned her head on the pillow, and forced open her heavy lids.

'I hate you for that,' she whispered.

And took Keel's mocking laugh with her into the darkness as the unaccustomed rum she had drunk earlier did its work, and released her to merciful oblivion.

CHAPTER TWO

Ros woke up feeling more human.

She pushed aside the blanket that covered her, and raised herself on a cautious elbow, but her head remained steady. So was the yacht, she discovered, which pointed to them being tied up somewhere.

She glanced at her watch. How long had she slept? The hands told her less than two hours, but her legs felt reassuringly firm as she tried her feet on the deck.

Her shoes and jacket were missing, so Keel must have taken them off, and her cheeks warmed at this evidence of his personal attention; but her confidence returned as she donned them and folded the blanket neatly back on to the bunk.

If the yacht had returned to Le Havre, she would go ashore and back to Paris, she decided, and wait at the airport for however long it took for the dispute to be settled, rather than risk a return of seasickness.

Grasping her handbag, she hurried on to the deck, ready to do battle with Keel if he should try to put obstacles in her way. He was on shore. She spotted him immediately, talking to the driver of a low-slung car, but the place where it was parked was not on the hard of the harbour they had left behind a couple of hours ago.

Instead, the yacht appeared to be moored in a small

inlet off the coast, and green parkland stretched out on either side. Some distance away, Ros spied the outline of a small private plane parked on the green.

Keel looked up as she walked down the gangway. 'I thought you'd never surface. Now you're here, let's get going.' He waved Ros to the waiting car.

'If we'd hung around in Paris we should have been a lot later.' She resented his attitude. It was the air strike, not herself, that was responsible for the delay. 'I thought we were going by boat.' She frowned.

'It would take too long. We're going by air the rest of the way. If you hurry up we'll just about get there in time. We'll have a following wind.'

'What's the haste? I didn't know we were suppoed to arrive at any particular time.'

'Milly's exhibition opens at five o'clock, and I'm due to perform the ceremony.' Keel slanted her a keen look. 'At least your face is a more normal colour. I hope air travel doesn't have the same effect on you?'

'Air travel never upsets me.'

She had not travelled in such a small place before, though. Ros eyed it with some apprehension as they approached, and wondered if the chauffeur who drove the car was also the pilot.

The man unwittingly answered her question when he said, 'As soon as you're airborne, Mr Hennessy, I'll contact Jean-Jacques and give him your orders.'

'Do that.' Keel nodded, and handed Ros up into the plane, which she saw boasted two seats, with only sufficient room to accommodate the pilot and one passenger.

Keel made sure Ros was securely strapped in before

taking the pilot's seat himself, and remarking, 'Now you know why we couldn't bring our suitcases with us.'

He switched on the engine, and its noisy exuberance drowned out any reply Ros might have made as, at a signal from the chauffeur, the little machine picked up speed and ran lightly over the grass.

It tilted skywards, and they were airborne, and, once Ros had overcome the initial strangeness of travelling in a Lilliputian-sized aircraft, she settled back and began to enjoy the ride.

The journey gave her time for conjecture.

The noise of the engine precluded conversation. Ros soon tired of watching the scenery below them, and looked inwards instead at her own thoughts which, no matter how she tried to deflect them, insisted upon centring themselves round her present companion.

Who was this man, she wondered, who could leave their luggage in one of the best hotels in Paris with the casual instruction to forward it on to them in Majorca? Who could commandeer an ocean-going yacht, and a private jet, however small, for his own purpose, and prove himself supremely competent to handle both? To say nothing of being asked to open an exhibition for the famous artist at the end of the journey. Even being a friend of the family did not give him sufficient standing for that.

So he must be someone of note in something or other. But what?

Ros stared, puzzled, at the back of his head, and

noticed inconsequentially that his hair curled up in a tiny drake's tail at the nape. Her fingers itched to spring the curl, and she checked them hastily, gripping them together in her lap, and forced her mind to think of all the personalities currently making newspaper headlines.

Sport? Keel's athletic figure proclaimed him to be a sportsman, but somehow the image of a professional did not quite fit. Neither did the stage, although his looks would more than qualify him to be an actor.

Politics? Ros dismissed politics out of hand.

Of one thing she felt convinced. He was not one of the hangers-on of whom Lyn had been so concerned. Her brief acquaintance with Keel was enough to tell Ros that he did not need to hang on to anyone. He was quite capable of taking charge of his own life, and anyone else's as necessary, evidence the way in which he had taken charge of herself. His bearing, his authoritative manner, the very cut of this clothes, spoke of wealth and confidence, and a supreme independence of anyone or anything.

She was no nearer to a solution when Keel called over his shoulder, 'Majorca's just ahead of us.'

The plane dipped a wing in a long bank, and green trees set in orderly rows on rich red soil took the place of the puff-balls of cloud that had made the journey in the small plane bumpy now and then.

Almond trees. Ros gazed down at them pensively. They had been in bloom the last time she visited Majorca on holiday. White bloom for the bitter almonds, she remembered, and pink blooms for the sweet nuts. Now, the trees would be bearing their crop. It was difficult to believe that she had left frost-bare branches behind her in England.

The island lay like a jewel below them, exquisitely set in Mediterranean blue. The plane pointed its nose towards a busy aerodrome, and the radio crackled, giving instructions from the control tower in Spanish, to which the pilot replied in words equally fluent while he obediently turned the machine in a circle, awaiting his turn to land.

A range of hills appeared under Ros's window, and then the waters of a wide bay. They were low enough now for her to be able to make out individual yachts among the vast shoal tied up neatly at their moorings, evidence of the countless yacht clubs that made the island a rich man's playground.

Their lack of luggage hastened their passage through the airport formalities, and Keel took Ros's arm and said, 'This way. There'll be a taxi waiting for us outside.'

He seemed to take it for granted that everything would be laid on to smooth his path, just as he had taken the yacht and the private jet for granted, and Ros's mind was in a whirl as she went along with him.

Events had happened so quickly that she was beginning to feel as if she was losing touch with reality. Since receiving the letter from Lyn, she had been pitchforked into a series of unexpected happenings at a speed that left her no time to grasp them, let alone to think, and having Keel as her escort was like being taken in charge by a whirlwind.

A man approached them as they emerged from the

airport building. 'Mr Hennessy? I've got instructions to take you to the art exhibition, sir.'

Keel slanted a glance at the expression on Ros's face, and his lips lifted.

'Welcome to the Isle of Calm, Ros.'

'The isle of what?' This was the first time Ros had heard the description, and in her present company it was anything but apt.

'Majorca has two names in the local dialect, *senora*.' The driver smiled as he opened the cab door for her. 'Some call it the Isle of Calm; others, the Isle of Dreams.'

'*Senorita*,' Ros corrected him hastily.

Her colour rose as she met Keel's sardonic look. It was a natural mistake on the driver's part, seeing them arrive together, but it was one that she did not intend to continue, even for the brief period of a taxi ride. She ignored Keel's derisive murmur, 'Nice to have a choice of two names,' that could have applied to the island or to herself, and dived into the shadowy interior of the cab to hide her glowing cheeks.

Calm was the last thing she felt as she renewed her acquaintance with the island, and if the speed of events of the last few hours was to continue, any dreams she might have were likely to be very disturbed ones indeed.

It was hot. Ros shrugged out of her jacket, and regretted her abandoned luggage. 'Can't we go the Casa Mimosa first and freshen up?' she asked.

'There isn't time. The Casa's on the other side of the island, and we've only got ten minutes to get to the exhibition.'

At Keel's urging, it was slightly less when the taxi halted in front of an imposing-looking building, its front liberally adorned with placards advertising the event.

Keel produced a gold-edged business card and gained instant entry for them both. The large room inside was packed with people, and he was greeted from every side as he took her arm and invited, 'Come and meet Milly.'

The artist proved to be refreshingly ordinary, but Ros could see at a glance why Lyn had been so concerned about her godmother. The rumpled appearance of Mildred Fisher's clothes, and her dreamy eyes, were evidence that their owner's thoughts were fixed elsewhere, and when Keel explained their last-minute arrival she said vaguely, 'How exciting. But surely you're not late? Is that really the time? I'd no idea.'

'You'll have to lend Ros a nightie,' Keel warned. 'We had to leave our luggage at the Cher. It'll probably be a couple of days before it catches up with us.'

'I wear pyjamas, but I don't expect you'll mind.'

'It's very kind of you, Miss Fisher.'

'Call me Milly. Everybody does.'

The artist waved a hand towards the gathering at large, and Ros noticed with an inward smile that there was a dab of vermilion paint on her wrist as if she had hurriedly washed her hands at the last minute, too absorbed in her work to spare much time, even for her own exhibition.

Milly took Keel's arm. 'Let's get the formalities over so that we can talk about something more interesting.' She smiled at Ros. 'Just circulate and enjoy yourself, my dear. We can talk later. Go round and have a look at the paintings, if you like that sort of thing.'

Clearly she did not mind if Ros did not care for her work, which was a relief. Ros had attended a few such exhibitions, and found it almost impossible to differentiate between the weird exhibits and the garish wallpaper behind them.

Mildred Fisher's paintings proved to be in an entirely different class.

Unusually for her, Ros saw that the artist worked in two media, both oil and watercolour, and was a master—or mistress—of both.

The oils were bold. Large seascapes filled the frames, and dramatic rock formations, many of which Ros recognised as being from Majorca itself.

The watercolours were gentler, delicately washed with a sensitive brush. Ros envied the people who could afford such gems, but the marked prices put them beyond her own reach.

One pillar was hung with miniatures, and she gasped with delight at the tiny exquisites; all portraits, she saw with interest, and all the subjects possessing the same characteristic, extraordinary beauty.

None of these was for sale. Perhaps they were commissioned portraits, or painted for the artist's own pleasure? Maybe the sitters were either family, or friends?

Was Keel's face among them? Before Ros could search the assembled miniatures to find out, Keel's voice rang out from the far side of the room.

'Ladies and gentlemen . . .'

He performed the opening ceremony with polished ease, and once again Ros found herself wondering who, and what, he was.

Amid loud applause he declared the exhibition open. Waiters began to circle the room offering light refreshments, and Ros suddenly realised that she was ravenously hungry. She had lost her breakfast, missed her lunch, and it was now rapidly approaching dinner time, with no guarantee of anything to eat until after the exhibition closed at goodness knew when. Not then, if Milly was as careless about meals as she was about her appearance, Ros thought ruefully; as a precautionary measure she waylaid a passing waiter.

A liberal mixture of titbits later, she captured a cup of coffee and drifted back towards Keel and Milly. They were talking to a tall, slender girl with black hair and black eyes which, Ros realised uncomfortably, were fixed on her with an insolent stare.

She hesitated, unwilling to intrude on the trio, but as she turned away Milly saw her, and called her over.

'Come and meet Una. Una, my dear, this is Ros. I told you about her.'

Whoever Una had been expecting, clearly it was not someone remotely like Ros. The meeting seemed to come as much of a shock to the other girl, as her own had been with Keel. Ros noted the startled look on Una's face as Milly went on,

'Would you believe, Una's the daughter of my best friend when I was at school? Such a sweet child.'

She must be referring to her school friend, Ros decided drily. The look Una directed at herself was the reverse of sweet. The black sloe eyes held all the malevolence of a spiteful child, and Ros could only think that the other girl's antagonism must stem from having another younger, and extremely good-looking, woman suddenly appear on what she regarded as her own territory.

She must be about Keel's age, Ros judged, making Una several years her own senior. Several decades her senior in experience, she judged shrewdly, schooling her face to hide her aversion to the newcomer.

Una had no need to worry so far as she was concerned. If Keel was her target, she was more than welcome. She, Ros, was on Majorca to earn her living, and she wanted her visit to pass as peacefully as possible.

A hopeless ambition anywhere within Keel's orbit. She felt she had had more than enough of his overbearing ways and, although she acknowledged he had achieved his objective, and got them to Majorca when otherwise they would still have been languishing at the airport in Paris, she felt as if it would take her the rest of her stay on the island to get her breath back.

'You and Una may have already met, while you were going round the exhibition,' Milly chatted on.

Una sneered, 'I saw you *eating* your way round the

exhibition.'

Ros coloured furiously. Hunger had obliged her to take full advantage of the refreshments on offer, lest her strength desert her before she reached the Casa, but Una's sneer inferred she was a professional meal scrounger.

What would Milly think? With an effort Ros forced back the hasty retort that rose to her lips. She would explain to Milly later. She owed no explanation to Una, and Keel already knew the reason behind her apparent self-indulgence.

She shot him a look which accused, 'You might have the decency to back me up,' but to her chagrin met only amusement in the amber eyes that watched the exchange with a lazy interest.

'You ought to eat something, too. You smoke too much, and don't eat half enough,' the artist scolded, but Una only tossed her head.

'I'm going back to the Casa. I've had enough of the crowds in here. Are you coming, Keel?'

She put out a possessive hand to draw him away, and Ros suppressed a smile when he resisted.

'I haven't had a chance to look at the paintings yet. You go on. I'll see you later.'

The black eyes flashed, but Una had driven herself into a corner from which there was no escape and, with a flounce that gave more than a hint of southern temper to match her colouring, she departed.

Milly said to Ros, 'You go and have another look at the paintings with Keel, my dear. Walsh Craythorne's driving me back home, and his car is only a two-seater.'

Keel said, 'Is he still around?' making Ros wonder who Walsh Craythorne was, and if he was one of the hangers-on, but Milly did not enlarge, merely saying,

'We eat on the terrace any time after seven,' before she drifted away and was lost in the crowd.

At least that would put a limit on the time she must spend with Keel, Ros thought thankfully. She wished someone would join them on their perambulation round the exhibition but, although a number of people spoke as they passed, and she was aware of more than one speculative glance following their progress, no one offered to accompany them.

'They're very good, aren't they?' Keel paused before one particular magnificent seascape.

'Fabulous.'

Why did the paintings seem so much more special the second time around? Ros wondered. Had Keel's company anything to do with it? She shied away from the explanation, and said hastily, 'I like the watercolours best.'

'They're Milly's favourites, too. She painted that one in an orange grove, close to the Casa Mimosa.'

Keel pointed to a painting gay with the colourful dresses of fruit-pickers busy in a laden grove, and so vivid was the interpretation that Ros could almost smell the fruit, and feel the hot sunshine.

'One of Milly's friends owns the estate, and we spent the day there, picnicking and helping with the harvest while Milly painted. It was great fun.'

Ros sent her companion a curious look. This was another side to this many-sided man. She could visualise him joining in the work, as at home among the fruit-pickers as he was at the wheel of the yacht, and piloting the plane.

Had Una been there, too? she wondered. If she had, Ros could not imagine the dark-haired sophisticate joining in with the fruit picking.

'That rock formation is in the mountains above the Casa, and that valley is below a monastery close by. We anchored the yacht and sunbathed while Milly captured the view of that headland.'

Keel brought each painting to life, unselfconsciously revealing a different world to Ros. A world in which yachts and private planes were taken for granted. A world in which Una belonged, and she herself definitely did not.

Sudden depression, that must have been the result of her hectic day, descended on Ros like a cloud as they neared the miniature paintings.

'Do any of the paintings appeal to you particularly?' Keel asked.

A note of unconscious wistfulness crept into her voice as Ros replied, 'Very much. The watercolour of the windmill and the wild flowers.'

It captured perfectly the paradox of the riverless island that was yet a garden of fruit and flowers, but like the other paintings it was beyond her reach. The miniatures would be more affordable, but they were not for sale.

'A lot of them are commissioned,' Keel told her. 'There should be one of Una somewhere among them. Here it is.'

It was Una as the artist saw her. A gentler, sweeter Una than the girl who was presented to Ros. If beauty was in the eye of the beholder, so was a nicer nature, Ros thought, and wondered who had commissioned the portrait. Had Keel?

Unaccountably the thought depressed her still further, and she felt a surge of relief when a chattering group of people came up to them and offered gaily, 'If you're carless, come back to the Casa with us. We've got a small minibus, and there's room for two more if we squeeze.'

To her consternation, Ros found herself squeezed against Keel, with five people occupying a seat that was only meant for three.

'Sit on one another's laps,' the driver suggested.

With twitching lips Keel agreed, 'That's a good idea,' and drew Ros down on to his own.

'Put me down,' she whispered confusedly.

'There isn't anywhere to put you, except on the floor.'

Scarlet-faced, Ros wished she could sink through the floor. Keel's arm held her firmly, and the unnerving effect it had had on her in the taxi seemed to double in intensity in the close physical contact of the minibus.

Ros tensed away from him, trying to hold herself upright in the speeding vehicle, but as the miles passed her muscles began to complain, and in spite of herself she was forced to give in and lean against Keel.

He grinned at her discomfiture, and Ros lashed herself for allowing it to show. He himself exhibited no sign of nerves; typically he remained in complete control of himself, and the situation.

'Are you comfortable?' he enquired calmly.

His breath zephyred her ear, and Ros hunched her shoulder against it, feeling it reach searching fingers down the length of her spine.

'Yes, thanks,' she lied. She knew that her tension must betray the effect he was having upon her, and his amusement showed in the deliberate tightening of his arm, making it worse.

The journey seemed to go on for ever.

The minibus climbed steadily over the mountain range on the west side of the island, along roads with hairpin bends so acute that they made Ros hold her breath.

The tarmac contortions tossed the other passengers around, but Keel held her firmly. She closed her eyes against the dizzy drops outside the bus windows, but with her lids shut she became even more vividly aware of Keel against her, so close that she could feel the even thump of his heart through the fine silk shirt that covered it. It seemed to vibrate through her body like an echo, bouncing back and forth through the emptiness that Lomas had left behind. Startled by her own reaction, Ros pulled herself upright.

'How far . . .' she stammered.

'We're nearly there. You can keep your eyes open now. We're over the worst bit of the road.'

It was a comfort that she could blame her nerves on the state of the road, and Ros heaved a small sigh of relief as the bus turned in through a pair of wrought-iron gates. 'This is the Casa Mimosa,' Keel said.

Milly must have reached home before them because, when Ros followed a young maid into her room, a pair of pyjamas was already neatly folded on her bed. They were clean and beautifully ironed, and faded to the point where scarcely a tint of their original colour showed.

But the brand new toothbrush and tube of toothpaste, and a hairbrush and comb likewise new, standing beside an unused tub of delicately perfumed talcum powder which Ros found put out for her use in the en suite bathroom, showed an unexpected thoughtfulness on the part of the artist, who must have stopped to purchase the small necessities on her way home.

Ros sought her out to thank her when she went downstairs.

'Think nothing of it,' Milly disclaimed. 'I'm afraid it's no use me lending you any day clothes. Most of mine are in the same state as my pyjamas, and they wouldn't look right on you.'

'Perhaps my luggage will come tomorrow.'

'No chance.' Keel came to join them. 'I've just heard the evening news bulletin on the television, and the strike looks as if it might be a long one. Both sides seem to be entrenched.'

'That settles it. You must go into town tomorrow and get yourself something pretty to wear,' Milly instructed.

'Won't you need me here?'

'Not until the evening. I want some things myself from the shops. I'll give you a list. And then after dinner you can sing to us. I do like nice singing, and Lyn told me you have a lovely voice.' She gave Ros a considering look. 'You have a lovely face as well. I long to put it on canvas.'

'Spare her tonight, Milly. The poor girl looks all in,' a voice protested. A stocky man with a Canadian accent, and eyes of the same iron grey as her hair, took Milly's arm, and smiled at Ros. 'Don't let her bully you. She forgets to eat or sleep when she's painting, and expects her models to do the same. Come to think of it,' the newcomer appealed to Keel, 'don't you think it would be a good idea if Milly went along on this shopping trip as well? Most of what she wears is just asking for a decent burial.'

If it had been Una speaking, the words would have been indescribably cruel. Coming from the man with the grey eyes, they were teasing, affectionate and completely bereft of hurt. Without being told, Ros knew this must be Walsh Craythorne, and she liked him on sight.

Milly made a face at him. 'My clothes suit me well enough. Come and let me tell you about my latest idea for a picture before everybody starts interrupting me with food.'

Milly drew Walsh and Keel away to a corner of the terrace where a canvas chair was surrounded by a litter of sketching materials, and Ros was left standing on her own. She was about to follow them when Una sidled up to her.

Her eyes swept critically over Ros's clothes, and instinctively she sprang to the defence of her inappropriate dress.

'We had to leave our luggage behind in Paris, because of the strike.'

She regretted the words the moment they were

spoken. She had no need to defend her actions to Una, but it was too late to retract, and her innocent use of the words 'we' and 'our', linking her with Keel, acted as a goad to Una. The full lips curled.

'How very convenient,' she sneered.

Ros's colour rose. 'It's the opposite to convenient so far as I'm concerned. This sweater's much too hot. But we couldn't bring our suitcases on Keel's small plane, so he left them at the Cher, of all places.'

'Naturally he'd leave them at the Cher. He owns the place.'

'He *owns* it?' Ros's eyes widened.

'Of course he does. He owns similar hotels in all the capitals. In fact, he owns a third of the hotels on this island. Don't tell me you didn't know?'

'Of course I didn't know. Why should I?'

Now Ros knew, it explained a good deal. Could it also explain Una's antagonism towards herself? she wondered. As owner of the Cher, and a string of similar top-grade hotels, to say nothing of being young and extremely good-looking, Keel was an eligible match.

'I expect you think it's worth putting up with the discomfort, when you know Milly's bound to buy you some more clothes at her expense.'

'It certainly is not, and I know nothing of the sort,' Ros exclaimed, taken aback by the other girl's attack.

'I heard Milly tell you to go into town tomorrow.'

'So what? She won't pay for my clothes.'

'Perhaps you'd like Keel to pay for them instead? Isn't that what you're angling for?'

Ros exploded indignantly, 'I'm not angling for

anything!'

'Or anybody?' Una's contemptuous look disbelieved her.

'Or anybody.'

Hot anger rose in Ros at the other girl's effrontery, but she refused to be drawn into a quarrel, which Una was patently trying to provoke.

'Just so long as you remember that——' Una's cigarette in its long holder stabbed in Ros's direction, underlining her words '—because Keel's already spoken for.' The words were a hissed threat, and the black eyes watched for Ros's reaction. When none came she shrugged. 'In any case, Keel's enough a man of the world to avoid being caught by a fortune-hunter.'

'How dare you!' Ros's voice shook, and her resolution to keep the peace wavered. This was in-fighting with a vengeance, and she had done nothing to justify the other girl's attack. 'If Keel's afraid of fortune-hunters, it isn't me he should avoid,' she lashed back. 'If I did have the misfortune to catch him, as you so crudely put it, I'd unhook him and throw him right back again.'

'Are you two girls coming to eat?' Keel's voice enquired from behind them, and they both spun round.

Ros caught her breath. How much had he heard of what she had said? She had allowed her anger against Una to push her into hasty speech, and if Keel had heard her remark, she had probably made an enemy of him as well. The sly glint of triumph in Una's eyes told her, too late, that the other girl had seen Keel approaching, and that the pushing had been deliberate, and successful.

Ros felt as if the entire day was using her as a pawn for its own malignant ends. Too late, she wished she had refused Lyn's plea to take her place at the Casa, but at the time it had seemed the balm she needed for the soreness Lomas had left behind. Now, it appeared as if the cure might prove more painful than the ill it sought to alleviate.

During the meal Ros could feel Una's antagonism flowing across the table towards her, and she leaned back in her chair and used Keel's bulk to shield her from the malicious currents. Una monopolished the conversation with Keel, and as soon as they reached the coffee stage she jumped up and cried,

'I'm bored. Let's put a tape on, and dance.'

Immediately there was an answering scramble from among the younger diners, who comprised the majority of the guests. Tables and chairs were pushed back, and people began to jig to the raucous music that issued from a loudspeaker at the end of the terrace.

'Turn the volume down, Una, do,' Walsh begged, but, if she heard the Canadian's plea, Una took no notice, pulling Keel with her to join in the dancing, if that was a fair description of the muscular spasms that contorted the performers, Ros thought critically.

She herself loved dancing, but saw little grace to commend the display going on in front of her. The over-loud music set a pulse throbbing painfully in her head, and she put up a hand to her temple.

The slight movement attracted Milly's attention,

and she said, 'I'll introduce you to the guests tomorrow, when you're rested. I don't know all of them myself. Most of the couples dancing are Una's friends. She likes having them here and, with her marriage splitting up, she needs some distraction; and she does enjoy entertaining.'

Doubtless, at Milly's expense. Watching Una, Ros thought the artist's anxiety on the girl's behalf was misplaced. The distraction Una sought was, quite obviously, Keel.

The girl's dancing was as blatant as a courting display in the wild, and it was shamelessly aimed at her wealthy partner. Her black eyes glittered up into his face, her hair tossed, and the sinuous movements of her arms slid her off-the-shoulder top low to a point of questionable modesty.

Clearly, being nearly rid of one husband, Una was going all out to net another, and from the verve with which he threw himself into responding, Keel did not seem averse to being made her captive.

The music rose to a cacophony of brass and drums, and Ros longed to press her hands over her ears when, with a suddenness that was almost shocking, it ceased. Into the silence Keel said clearly, 'Let's give our ears a break, shall we?' betraying his own hand as the one that had manipulated the switch.

Una looked furious at the interruption, but Milly sent Keel a grateful look. 'I'm afraid my taste in music isn't very modern,' she said apologetically.

'Ros will sing you something more to your liking,' Keel answered, and his look at Ros was a command.

Resentment flared in Ros. Walsh Craythorne was

more considerate. He had seen how tired she was, and warned Milly off asking anything of her tonight. Keel had no such compunction.

He of all people should have been aware of the extent of her tiredness. He had seen her collapse from seasickness; he had dragged her on a hectic succession of taxis, train, boat and plane, and now he apparently expected her to sing as if she had done nothing all day.

Did he drive everyone as hard as he drove himself? Ros longed to refuse. Keel was not her employer; Milly was. But if she refused, it would show weakness, and Keel would scorn her for it—and Una would triumph.

Pride came to Ros's aid; she would not give them that satisfaction. She hoped her tiredness would not show in her voice. She sang where she sat, sweetly and naturally, leaning back in her chair and letting the notes flow unaccompanied in a selection of ballads that ideally suited her husky contralto.

Momentarily she forgot her weariness, as she always did when she sang, losing herself in the joy of the music, and one ballad slipped into another in a repertoire that she herself loved, and knew intuitively that Milly would, too.

The last note throbbed into silence. It was as if the small audience held its breath, straining to catch the last lovely echo before it died away, and then someone started to clap, and Ros found herself surrounded.

'That was great.'

'Your voice is as beautiful as you are.'

'More! We must have more.'

Una did not join in the general adulation. She stood to one side biting her lip, and the expression on her face was not pleasant to see. Ros averted her eyes, and found them resting on Keel instead.

She could not see his expression. He leaned casually against the terrace balustrade, still in an attitude of listening, but his face was in shadow, giving nothing away.

'Encore! Encore!'

It grew to a chant, and Ros looked helplessly across at Milly. Now she had finished singing, the tiredness flooded back with renewed force. Dark bruises shadowed her eyes, and her face lost what little remaining colour it had.

Her condition registered even with Milly, who said firmly, 'No more now.' She raised a hand to silence the chorus of protest. 'Tomorrow evening, when Ros is rested, we'll ask her to sing again, but not tonight.' She turned to Ros, and her face was still lit with the pleasure of the singing.

'That was wonderful, my dear. You must sing for us every day while you're here. A fortnight isn't nearly long enough to enjoy hearing your beautiful voice. You must extend your stay for as long as possible.'

The catch of Una's breath was audible through the silence that followed Milly's invitation, and Ros rose to her feet, avoiding a direct reply.

'Of course I'll sing, as often as you want me to,' she promised, and with a general, 'Goodnight,' she escaped to her room.

Behind her, she heard Una's shrill demand, 'Now, for goodness' sake let's have something a bit livelier,' and the music started up again, but not, Ros noticed, as loudly as before.

Even so, she closed her window against the sound before she dropped into bed, but although she closed her eyes she could not shut out the questions that came to disturb the sleep she needed so badly.

If Milly repeated her invitation to extend her stay at the Casa, should she accept? Or should she insist upon remaining for only the two weeks originally agreed upon?

If she left at the end of the fortnight, she would be denying herself much-needed employment, but if she remained at the Casa she knew that Una would do everything in her power to make life impossible, and the ensuing cross-currents and tensions would send her back home with her nerves as jangled as when she started out.

Drowsily, her mind drifted to Keel. Would he want her to remain, or not? Or wouldn't he care either way?

It did not affect her whether he cared or not, but, as Ros drifted off to sleep, her dreaming mind still sought to find the answer in his shadowy face.

CHAPTER THREE

ROS sought out Milly at breakfast the next morning and asked, 'Is there a bus into town from the village?'

The day had dawned hot, and she had coiled her hair round her head in a desperate search for whatever relief she could find. The quicker she could exchange her sweater and skirt for a cotton outfit, the better.

Ros blessed the fact that she always made a point of carrying her travellers' cheques on her person, and not in her suitcase, which would have put her in the embarrassing position of having to borrow money from Milly. After Una's remarks the evening before, that was the last thing she wanted to do.

'Go in the minibus,' Milly answered.

Ros looked doubtful. 'My driving isn't up to coping with that road over the mountains.'

'You won't be driving. I will.' Keel overheard her, and came to join them. 'I'm going into town this morning to bring back any unsold paintings from the exhibition. Not that there are likely to be many.' He smiled at his hostess.

'So sweet of you, Keel, to do this for me. I'm absolutely hopeless at the business side of things.'

'Don't we know it. You'd give a Goya to the doorman for a tip.' Walsh laughed, and took the artist by her arm. 'Come for a walk with me before it gets too hot.'

'You're always taking me off for a walk in the morning, just when the light's at its best.'

'If I don't catch you before you lose yourself in your latest painting, I'd never get you on your own at all.'

'Oh, well, if you must.'

Milly did not seem averse to leaving her painting to walk with Walsh, Ros noticed. 'I'll try,' she promised, when Milly said, 'Get yourself something pretty when you're in town. We're celebrating tonight.'

The couple strolled off together, and Keel said, 'We'll go, too, before you cook in that outfit.'

'It's a bit late for you to feel concerned about my comfort. You could have given me time to take one or two things out of my suitcase. A couple of dresses wouldn't have taken up much room.'

The stifling discomfort of her sweater sharpened Ros's voice. She should have insisted upon bringing some things with her, but Keel had rushed her off her feet at such a speed that her thinking powers had deserted her, and she was suffering the consequences now.

'There wasn't time. If we'd missed the train, we would have missed the tide.'

'From where I stand, that wouldn't have been a bad thing.'

Keel's lips lifted. 'Your stomach didn't take kindly to the sea.'

Ros ignored his gibe. Her nerves had not taken too kindly to the journey over the mountains, either, and she viewed the return trip with a lively apprehension.

Once inside the minibus, however, her nerves stemmed from a different source. She was acutely aware of Keel sitting close beside her. He changed gear, and his arm brushed against her own. Ros pulled hastily out of his way, but the tingle of his touch remained like an irritant on her skin as he leaned back in his seat, totally relaxed, in a manner Ros envied but could not emulate.

He coaxed the vehicle round the hairpin bends of the mountain road in a way that never once disturbed her balance as the driver of yesterday had done to his passengers, but Ros would have preferred that kind of disturbance to the one that afflicted her now.

Although she remained outwardly cool, inside her stomach was aflutter with nerves. All her feminine instincts reacted to Keel's virile masculinity like the attraction of steel to a magnet, and her efforts to restrain them left her feeling jangled, and irritable with herself.

When Keel parked the car in front of the building that had housed the exhibition the day before, she decided on escape. She did not want Keel's company while she shopped. If the way he had taken control of her until now was any guide, he would probably expect to dictate what she bought, and from where. The shops Keel could afford to patronise would be very different from those Ros had in mind.

She opened the car door. 'Thanks for the lift. I'll leave you to deal with Milly's paintings, and join you later. What time?'

'In exactly five minutes.'

'Five minutes?' Ros stared. 'I can't possibly shop in that time. I've got a list of things to get for Milly, as well as . . .'

'I don't expect you to. You couldn't get to the main shopping centre in that time; it's nearly a mile away from here. Just stay in your seat while I go into the gallery and let the people know we're here, so that they can load the crate or whatever into the back. Then we can go and park at the Dinaldo, and do our shopping from there.'

'He owns a good third of the hotels on this island . . .'

Of course, he would probably own the Dinaldo as well, and could be sure of a parking space in the crowded town centre. Ros's forehead creased as she settled herself back into her seat.

As soon as they were parked at the hotel, she must find an excuse to lose Keel. If her memory served her correctly, the Dinaldo stood in the centre of the equivalent to London's Bond Street and, while Ros enjoyed window shopping in the luxurious stores, their prices, like the paintings, were far beyond her reach.

Keel would need to buy clothes for himself, though. The thought brought her instant relief. He had left his own suitcase behind at the Cher as well, so he, too, could only have the clothes he stood up in, and would go his own way to get replacements when they reached the shopping centre.

At the Dinaldo, Keel pulled the minibus into a reserved car parking space bearing his name on a wall plate, and confirming Ros's guess that he must be the owner. He spoke in rapid Spanish to a man in attendant's uniform who hurried across.

'Si, Senor Hennessy.' The attendant took Keel's ignition key and went away, and the latter said,

'If we turn left here, there's a store at the corner of the street where you'll be able to get everything you need under one roof.'

'I'd rather have a look round first. I'll meet you back at the minibus, shall we say in an hour's time?'

Ros's fears as to Keel's choice of a store came to a head as they turned left and were confronted by black marble pillars and plate-glass doors with the name of the store enscrolled across them in letters of black and gold. It was the most exclusive in the whole of the shopping area.

'If you want to look round the store opposite, you'll take for ever to get served.' Keel nodded towards the large multiple with the gaily dressed windows, into which at that moment poured the contents of at least four coachloads of tourists.

Ros's heart sank.

The multiple would have served her purpose admirably. Its clothes were of good quality, at reasonable prices, and would have seen her through the days until her luggage caught up with her. So long as she had suitable clothes to wear, Milly would not expect her to appear in *haute couture*.

Ros smiled at the thought of Milly in connection with *haute couture*, but the next thought wiped the smile from her face. Keel was not a man to be kept waiting, and she would be last in a queue of goodness knew how long, if she went into the store opposite.

'I'll have to change a traveller's cheque first.' She made one last attempt to break free from him, but he dismissed her excuse as easily as he had the others.

'The store will do all that's necessary.'

With a mental shrug Ros gave in. Keel had the transport, so he had the whip hand. She would go with him, and buy only the minimum amount of clothes necessary. She could spend up to the amount of her traveller's cheques and afterwards she would have to rely on what little money she had left in her purse, and the money Milly was to pay her for her work at the Casa.

She would have preferred to save those earnings as a cushion for when she returned home. Ros knew she would be assured of a welcome at her parents' house in the small market town where her father was the local vet, but she preferred to remain independent. Her two younger brothers were still respectively at university and college, and she was determined not to be a further drain on the family income.

In spite of her reservations, she could not restrain a feeling of delicious anticipation as she went with Keel between the imposing marble pillars, and into the perfumed air of the store.

Lovely clothes were a delight to wear, and if she shopped carefully she would leave Majorca with souvenirs *extraordinaires*, to treasure and enjoy for a long time to come.

She soon completed Milly's list of shopping, and followed Keel to the escalator which directed them to

'Men's department, first floor. Ladies' fashions, second floor'.

'Why is it that stores always make women climb an extra floor?' she exclaimed crossly. 'It's sheer chauvinism.'

'Because they know the fair sex will go to any lengths to gild the lily.' Keel helped her on to the moving stairway.

'Men won't, I suppose?' she shot over her shoulder, and was taunted by his laugh from behind her.

At the top of the escalator Ros turned to mount the next flight upwards, and to her consternation found Keel still beside her.

'I can find my own way,' she protested. Did he imagine she was so naïve that she might lose herself? 'You get your own clothes. I'll join you later.'

'I don't need clothes.'

'You must need some. You left your own suitcase at the Cher.'

'I keep a spare set of clothes on Majorca. I have to come to the island quite often, and it saves the bother of bringing luggage everytime.'

'You had luggage with you in Paris.'

'Only because I was on my way back from a long stay down under. I've got everything I need here.' He saw her significant glance sweep the slacks and shirt he had on yesterday. 'My clothes are kept at the Dinaldo. I've instructed the car park attendant to see that a selection from my wardrobe is packed and put into the minibus for when we return. So you'll have all the time to choose whatever you want for yourself.'

His presence was thoroughly off-putting. With Keel looking over her shoulder, Ros found it embarrassing to study the price tags as closely as her limited funds demanded. Surreptitiously she converted pesetas into pounds, and winced at the answers she got.

Those garments that were unpriced, she returned to the racks, alerted by their appearance as to what their cost might be. Keel had sharp eyes, she discovered, when she returned the second.

'That long violet dress is the exact colour of your eyes. Don't you like it?'

'I don't need it.' She had picked it from the rack for no other reason than to enjoy looking at it.

'What does need matter, if you like it?'

It mattered everything to Ros's limited funds, but she would die rather than admit it to Keel. She tightened her lips and returned the dress firmly to the rack, and Keel showed open impatience at her stubbornness.

'You'll be here all day at this rate. There must be something you like among all this lot.'

There was a lot Ros liked, mostly among the unpriced garments, and including the long violet dress, which she saw at a glance would be a perfect fit, but she turned her back on it and added it to her list of dreams, along with the watercolour painting of the windmill and the wild flowers.

'If you're in such a hurry, why did you bother to bring me?'

Probably because Una was not up in time to come

with him, Ros silently answered her own question, settling at random for a gay cotton skirt and a couple of tops, along with a pair of cream slacks that would go with either, and a cotton dress that was pretty enough to do duty for both afternoons and evenings.

'You must have something long for this evening,' Keel said. 'Remember Milly's celebrating the success of her exhibition.'

Ros had forgotten. She had not given Milly's remark more than a passing thought, since the artist's own mode of dress was casual to say the least, and she had assumed that what she had chosen would cope with any eventuality at the Casa until her own luggage arrived.

Her selection of clothes would eat up a good half of her stock of traveller's cheques, she realised with dismay, without adding an evening dress to it. Cautiously she chose a long cotton skirt instead, but the price of even that made her blanch, although she refused to allow her consternation to show in front of Keel.

Alone in the changing-room she did some quick mental arithmetic. The slacks would have to go. Even without them, she would have only the equivalent of about five pounds in English money left. She gave them back to the assistant, and began to try on the rest.

Outside the cubicle she could hear Keel's voice ask, 'May I see?' and the assistant's reply, 'I'll go and find out.'

The cubicle door opened a crack, and the girl turned with a smile. 'The *señora's* dressed.'

Ros compressed her lips. *'Señorita,'* she muttered. This was the second time she had been mistaken for Keel's wife.

She met Keel's mocking look in the cubicle mirror as he came in to appraise her freshly attired form, and she tingled under his look.

'Hmm. Very nice,' he opined.

Damning with faint praise. Ros's irritation erupted. 'Go away and let me get changed, and we can go back to the Casa.'

'There's no haste.'

'Now you tell me.' She turned her back on him.

'Do you want me to help you with the zips?'

'No!'

Ros spun back again. She saw that he was laughing at her, and hated him for it, and for the things he was doing to her self-possession. Keel possessed an uncanny ability to scrabble her composure, and knew it; he took a fiendish delight in striking sparks off her whenever the opportunity presented itself, which was a lot too often for Ros's liking.

'Get out!' she gritted.

He went with a mocking smile that made Ros long to slam the door after him. She folded her own clothes with hands that shook and kept on the short cotton skirt and top, unconscious of the fact that the summery outfit pared several years off her age and, with her braided hair, gave her a look of demurity that made Keel's eyes kindle as she rejoined him.

She felt cooler and more in control of herself, now that she was dressed in more suitable clothes. As she took the exclusive-looking carrier from the assistant, the girl smiled and turned away, and Ros called after her;

'My bill?'

'That's been taken care of, *señorita.*'

'Taken care . . .' Ros pivoted to stare at Keel.

'That's right.' He took her by the arm and began to draw her away.

Ros glared at him furiously. She could not argue with him in the store, as he must be very well aware, but she was unable to restrain her anger at his action.

'How dare you pay my bill?' Men who bought girl acquaintances expensive wardrobes expected to be paid in kind. How dared he assume she was that kind of girl? Her low voice was filled with outrage. 'I buy my own clothes. I'll pay you back every penny the moment we reach the Casa.'

'They're pesetas, not pennies. And it's Milly you owe the money to, not me.'

That made it marginally better, but not much.

Keel went on, 'Milly told me before we started out this morning to charge whatever you bought to her account here.'

'Milly's got an account *here?*'

The idea was so incongruous that Ros was taken aback. Keel grinned at her expression.

'Milly does dress up, on occasion. We tease her about her clothes. When she's working, she forgets everything except her painting. But now and then she takes a break. You'll see, she'll appear in all her finery for the celebration tonight.'

And to make sure Ros did not disgrace the gathering, Keel had steered her into buying something appropriate. She did not know whether to feel mortified, or grateful. Impatiently shrugging aside either, she reiterated,

'I'll pay Milly as soon as we get back. I'm not here to gold-dig, no matter what you might think.'

'I don't think anything of the kind.' His face hardened.

'Una does. She told me so last night.'

'Una says things she doesn't mean, on the spur of the moment.'

Una had meant that, and it was not a spur-of-the-moment remark. It was a calculated, pre-meditated insult and, no matter how Keel excused the other girl, Ros had no intention of justifying her sneer.

If the artist refused her offer of the money, she decided, she herself would refuse to accept her salary at the end of her fortnight's stay, and the one would cancel out the other.

They reached the Dinaldo and Keel said, 'Give your parcel to the commissionaire. He'll put it in the minibus while we have our lunch.'

'Aren't we going back to the Casa right away?'

'I told you there was no haste.'

Ros had got quite the reverse impression from his impatience with her in the store. She assumed Keel must want to go back to the Casa to be with Una, and the manner in which he had allowed the girl to monopolise him last night lent strength to her assumption. Keel would not allow anyone to monopolise him if he did not want them to.

During the meal, however, he dropped his authoritarian manner and became the perfect host. He chatted casually, careful not to mention the controversial shopping, and, under his relaxed approach, little by little Ros began to relax, unconsciously lowering her guard against him.

To her surprise she found she was enjoying the delicately flavoured soup which he had ordered, and the tiny grilled sardines that followed, accompanied by crusty rolls and a rich tomato dip.

Roast suckling pig, and fresh young vegetables that were still a dream of summer to come at home, were accompanied by a wine that was clean and fresh on her palate, leaving it free afterwards to savour the newly picked strawberries with the taste of the sun in each juicy bite.

Have you seen the outdoor market here?' Keel enquired when they reached the coffee stage. Ros answered, regretfully, 'No. When I came on holiday, there wasn't time to fit it in.'

'It's market day today. When we've finished, we'll have a look around.'

The authority was back, and Ros's resentment returned with it. She had had perforce to put up with Keel telling her what to do during their journey to the island, but she did not intend it to become a habit.

'I haven't got time to look round markets,' she refused. 'I must go back. I'm here to work, not to go sightseeing.'

'Milly won't need you until this evening. She said so.' How typical of Keel to remember that, and use it to thwart her.

'Just the same . . .' Ros began stubbornly.

'You can't go back to the Casa without me,' Keel

interrupted, 'because there's no public transport. I'm going to have a look round the market while we're here. It's up to you whether you come with me, or stay here by yourself.'

Their glances met and clashed across the table, tawny determination doing battle with violet rebellion.

'Please yourself,' Keel clipped.

If she pleased herself, she would have nothing more to do with this impossibly domineering, and disturbingly attractive man.

But if she remained in the hotel by herself, she would be conspicuous in a restaurant that was rapidly emptying. The lunch period was over, the staff would be going off duty until after their usual *siesta* time, and she had no idea how long Keel was likely to be away. If she defied him, he was quite capable of keeping her hanging about for hours, just to punish her. Ros bit her lip.

'Would you like something more, sir?' The waiter hovered, wanting to clear the table.

'No, thanks. We're going now. I'll collect my car keys from reception when we come back.'

Keel rose, and Ros had no option but to rise with him. Her chagrin knew no bounds that he had over-ridden her yet again, and there was nothing she could do about it.

The streets outside the hotel were thronged with tourists, making it impossible to argue with Keel as he steered her through the crush, taking full advantage of it to silence her, she realised angrily.

He slipped through the knots of craning sightseers

with an adroitness and speed that left Ros breathless
and reduced her to begging, 'Slow down,' as they
turned up a steep, cobbled alleyway leading off the
main thoroughfare.

Keel slowed obligingly. 'The market's at the top of
the alley.'

Ros would not have found it by herself. Its entrance
was hidden between two shop fronts, and few except
those thoroughly conversant with the area would
know that it was a through passage.

It was dim and cool, so narrow that the wrought-
iron balconies almost met overhead and shut off the
glare of the sun. Except for herself and Keel, and a
mongrel stretched under an almond tree that
sprouted from among the cobbles, it was deserted.

If she had been alone Ros would have ventured no
further, but with Keel's reassuring height beside her
she revelled in this snippet of the old Majorca hidden
away behind the bustling facade of a modern
shopping street.

Pot plants trailed like coloured lace from every
balcony, reaching across the shuttered windows that
gave the houses a withdrawn and secretive air. The
sound of water drew her eyes to a tiny fountain
playing in a marble courtyard, from which rose a
stairway with more wrought iron guarding its steps,
but of people there was no sign.

A secret place indeed.

The contrast with the crowds they had left behind
was almost eerie, and instinctively Ros shrank closer
to Keel's side. He looked down at her, and his eyes
were amused.

'There's nothing to be afraid of. It's *siesta* time for the locals; that's why it's deserted. Only the tourists like the sun.'

There was an obscure something in his peaty glance that made Ros vaguely afraid of something that had nothing to do with the deserted alley. Was it of herself? She gave an unexpected shiver, and to cover it up said quickly; 'The tourists will soon have to do without the sun, from the look of that black cloud over there.'

They emerged into the wide market square just as the sun went in, and a chill breeze rippled through the wares hung on the market stalls, jutifying her shiver.

Lace tablecloths, and clothes and draperies of every description, began to flap and sway in the rapidly strengthening breeze, and Keel looked down at Ros and said, 'You're chilly. Didn't you bring your sweater with you?'

'No, I left it in . . .' A loud clap of thunder drowned the rest of her sentence.

'Get under cover, quickly.' Keel propelled her under the canvas awning of the nearest market stall as the rain descended in a deluge of such ferocity as Ros had never encountered before. It hammered on the canvas stall cover, driven by a gusting wind that sent the hanging lace goods into a frenzied dance, but thanks to Keel's quick thinking, he and Ros remained dry.

However, the wind sucked every vestige of warm air from the marketplace, and what a few minutes before Ros had welcomed as a cool outfit now turned into an inadequate cover for her shrinking frame. Goose pimples raised along the length of her arms, and her teeth began to chatter.

'The *señora* is cold,' the stallholder observed alertly.

With his small space crammed with sheltering tourists, he took quick advantage of what the gods offered to push his wares.

'We have some shawls, *señora*,' he cajoled. 'Cotton or silk, or these cashmere ones. They're light, and warm . . .'

'No,' Ros gritted.

This was the third time she had been called *señora*, and her patience was at an end. The trader became persistent.

'The colours match your dress, *señora*.'

Ros could see the colours for herself. The shawls were rainbow hued, and beguilingly soft, and her eyes longed for their beauty as much as her shrinking body cried out to be wrapped in their cosy warmth.

Sternly she denied them both. She could not afford a shawl; she had only coppers in her purse.

'No,' she reiterated firmly.

'Yes,' Keel said, and pointed to a cashmere shawl in the palest violet.

Swift as a thought the trader hooked it down and the shawl changed hands. Ros flared, 'I won't . . .' but Keel turned her masterfully towards him and draped the delicate square over her head and shoulders, from where it reached down nearly to the hem of her skirt.

'You will,' he insisted, and his arms held it round her, trapping her own inside.

The delicate wool erased the goose pimples from her arms and stilled the shivers across her back, and Keel moulded her to him, using his own body to shield her front from the slicing wind.

Lightly clad himself, he seemed impervious to the chill, and warmth of a very different kind flowed from him to set Ros's veins alight. She caught her breath. It was like coming into contact with the glow of living coals.

She tried ineffectually to pull away from him, but the crowds hemmed her in, making movement impossible. Something deep inside her, and out of her control, began to stretch into life, as a seed is drawn to the warmth of the sun, regardless that it might perish in the fierce heat.

Helpless to prevent it, Ros sensed it grow and anger against this thing that she could not control grew with it. She burst out sharply, 'I don't accept gifts from strangers.'

'I'm not a stranger.'

How, then, did he regard himself? And her? His dancing eyes challenged her to guess, and Ros dropped her lashes, suddenly confused.

She did not want to be reminded that Keel had put her to bed when she was seasick on the yacht; had cradled her on his knee during the journey over the mountains to the Casa; and had taken her on an intimately personal shopping trip this morning, all of which put them on a very different footing from that of strangers.

She could feel his eyes watching her, lit by the glow of the coals that turned them into two bright orbs of living fire, boring down into her face, and reading the doubt and uncertainty that flitted across her mobile features.

'Give the shawl back,' she insisted. 'I don't want presents from you. You've got no right . . .'

'I've got every right to protect Milly's interests.'

'What's Milly got to do with it?'

'She enjoys your singing. If you get a sore throat, you won't be able to use your voice.'

He was unstoppable. He rode over her protests with the dreadful inevitability of an armoured vehicle demolishing a wooden stockade, and Ros watched her defences fall with a feeling akin to despair.

She longed to toss the shawl away, but the unnameable thing that flowered deep inside her drew the unwanted gift close round itself, and smiled. Through the turmoil of her thoughts, Ros heard a voice from another world cry, 'It's stopped raining. Let's go back to that other stall, and . . .'

She blinked and looked round her. It had, indeed, stopped raining. A gleam of strengthening sunshine split the last trailing edges of the cloud, and steam began to rise from the canvas of the stall. Keel dropped his hands from round her and said,

'We must be going, too. I've arranged to call back at the exhibition hall to pick up the man who organised Milly's display yesterday. He's coming to the Casa tonight to join in the celebrations with us.'

That must have been why Keel had come to look round the market, to kill time until he picked up his other passenger. Not in order to show her one of the sights she had not seen before.

The thing that was blossoming inside her began to shrivel, and lost its smile.

Perversely now Ros wanted to remain. The sun reappeared in all its former strength and brought the scene to life again, and she envied the tourists who had time to stop and stare, and buy. She turned in silence to walk beside Keel back to the minibus, only to find her way blocked by a gypsy woman, who stood four square in their path and wheedled, 'Buy a flower for the lady, for luck.'

They were obliged to stop, or walk over her.

Her face was as gnarled as the bark of the olive trees Ros had seen on their journey through the mountains, with lines like deep valleys criss-crossing skin that was almost as dark as the olives themselves. Black hair, still glistening with the rain, hung in tight braids below her waist, and the sun struck glints from gold chains at her neck and wrists.

Whatever beauty she had once possessed the sun had withered with the fierce heat of countless island summers, but she held herself erect with a majestic grace that scorned alike the years and the weather. Ros longed to capture her queenly figure on canvas, and wondered if Milly already had.

'Buy a flower . . .'

Ros fumbled in her purse, but women's lib had not yet penetrated the gypsy encampments of Majorca. The woman glanced at her, and away again, and fixed her penetrating black eyes on Keel.

'For the lady, for luck,' she intoned.

Keel dug into his pocket, and accepted the red carnation, and the gypsy moved on. Ros heard her call from somewhere among the crowd, 'Buy a flower for the lady.'

'For luck,' her mind finished the sentence for her.

She could do with some luck, she reflected ruefully. She was not superstitious, but . . . Would the flower work?

She caught her breath on a sudden thought. Keel might not give the flower to her. He might keep it, and give it to Una instead. Suddenly it became desperately important to Ros that Keel should give the carnation to herself. Without knowing why, she wanted the flower more than anything she had seen or purchased that morning.

It might bring her luck, she excused her unaccustomed avarice. She glanced at the carnation in Keel's fingers, and knew that there must be longing in her look for the single, simple flower. Knew, too, that Keel must see it, although he could not know the reason why she wanted it so badly, because she did not know it herself.

She knew that she did not want Keel to give it to Una.

The bright scarlet petals would look wild and wanton, and entirely fitting, in the other girl's dark hair, but it was for her, Ros, whom the gypsy had intended it, and she knew she would feel deprived, and furiously angry, if Keel gave it to Una instead.

'For the lady, for luck,' he mimicked, and slotted the slender stem in the braid of her hair.

Now he had given her the flower, for some unaccountable reason Ros wanted to cry. She blinked rapidly, and Keel smiled down at her and said, 'You should always wear a flower in your hair.'

Ros put up exploring fingers to touch it. The petals felt soft and delicate, still slightly damp from the storm, like tears newly dried. She dashed away her own, and smiled, and something that was as unaccountable as the tears bubbled up inside her, making her want to sing. It parted her lips, and irradiated her face, and the sun joined in as Keel scooped up her hand in his and said,

'Come on. Let's find our alley.'

Our alley . . . Mischief danced in Ros's eyes, and she began to sing softly, 'Sally, Sally . . .'

Keel laughed, enjoying the joke and, swinging hands lightheartedly, they ran together across the steaming puddles of the market square to find the entrance to the alley.

'Heavens, it's turned into a river.' Ros halted in her tracks, dismayed. Water ran down the steep cobbled slope, draining into the main shopping street in an inch high torrent that would fill her thin-soled court shoes within seconds.

The mongrel that had lain at ease under the almond tree passed them, shaking its coat disconsolately, and making for drier ground. Ros stretched out a foot tentatively to see if she could reach a group of cobblestones that sat higher then the rest, like a tiny island in the swirling water. If she could manage to hop from stepping stone to stepping stone . . .

'Don't get your feet wet.' Before Ros realised what he was about to do, Keel reached out and swung her up high into his arms, as if her weight was no more than that of a child.

The look in his eyes as they lanced down into her upturned face, so close under his chin, was the reverse of childlike, and a quiver ran through her as she lay in his arms.

Urgently she tried to wriggle herself free. 'Put me down.'

'Lie still, or I'll drop you in a puddle.'

He was quite capable of carrying out his threat. The water threatened her from below, and Keel's mouth laughed at her confusion from tantalisingly close above her.

He jumped from stone to stone, weighing the distance carefully between each stepping point so as not to slip, and each time he made a perfect landing, until he reached the almond tree.

It was the last, and longest jump of all. After the tree, the water channelled itself into a drainage groove in the centre of the alley, built into the cobbles for that purpose, but the distance from the stone on which Keel balanced, to dry ground under the tree, was almost twice what he had jumped previously.

In between, the water ran wide and deep and muddy, carrying with it grit and debris from the marketplace. If he misjudged his step, he would land calf deep in the unsavoury flow.

'Put me down,' Ros cried, but for all the notice Keel took of her she might as well not have spoken. With swift eyes he assessed the distance, and then he took off in a jump that reminded Ros of the lithe spring of a mountain lion.

Just so would a wild cat carry off its prey.

The simile sent a shockwave through her, and

another of a different kind followed hard on its heels. Keel landed lightly, but the cobble under his one foot was loose, and tilted under his weight. Quickly he leaned against the tree trunk to steady himself, and his weight shook down a shower of water from the leaves in a cold douche, straight into Ros's upturned face.

'Ugh! That was a wash I didn't expect.'

She dashed both hands across her eyes to clear them as Keel set her on her feet, and then turned to walk along the alley ahead of him. She had only taken one step, when his hand descended on her shoulder and spun her to face him.

'They're real,' he exclaimed in a surprised voice. 'The colour, I mean.'

'What's real?'

Why did he hold her so closely, searching her face as if it was some kind of map? The speed at which her pulse began to race was only too real. It brought a singing to her ears, and her throat felt tight with the effort of resisting his stare. Ros mumbled again, 'What's real?'

'The colour of your eyelashes.'

They widened in surprise at his unexpected answer. 'Of course they're real.'

'They're so dark, and your hair's so gold, I thought it must have been make-up. But if it was, it would have run after the wetting you've just had. Una's did, once, when she got a soaking.'

Ros's tension exploded in a helpless giggle. The thought of Una's face streaked with black make-up was irresistibly funny. And then her laughter died.

For Keel to discover that Una's make-up ran, his own face must have been very close to that of the other girl.

As close as his lips were to her own, now. They hovered, palpitatingly near, and Ros went deathly still as his hand came up round the back of her head, and tipped her face even closer.

'No wonder Milly wants to paint you. You're beautiful,' he muttered, and his lips closed the gap between them.

A shockwave passed over Ros. Endless seconds ticked by, filled with an eternity of experience that was like nothing she had known before. The green canopy of the almond tree waved above her head, and she wondered vaguely if it bore sweet or bitter nuts.

Bitter-sweet.

Sweet was the feel of Keel's lips exploring her own. A dangerous, beguiling sweetness that, if she was tempted to taste it, might offer a deadly draught, because Keel belonged to a world that was poles apart from her own.

Una's world.

Bitter was the knowledge that, by giving her the shawl and the carnation, casual gifts from a man to whom the cost was a mere bagatelle, he should assume it gave him the right to buy her kisses in return.

CHAPTER FOUR

ROS wrenched herself free from Keel's arms.

'I don't sell my kisses. Not for shawls, nor for flowers,' she spat furiously and, turning, ran blindly down the alley away from him, careless of the water or the slippery cobbles.

She could hear Keel's footsteps running behind her, gaining on her, and unreasoning panic built up inside her. She fled for the main shopping street where there would be crowds of tourists, and Keel would not be able to hold her, and kiss her, again.

Heedless of where she trod, she did not see the raised cobble in front of her, and the slender heel of her court shoe snagged in the gap between it and its fellow, snubbing her to a halt as her shoe twisted almost off her foot.

Keel caught her as she stumbled.

'You little fool. Do you want to break your ankle?'

'Let me go! Don't touch me.'

Her mind was in a turmoil, and his touch made the turmoil worse.

'What on earth's the matter with you? Haven't you ever been kissed before?'

Ros did not know what was the matter with her. Her feelings were in such confusion, she felt incapable of rational thought. She had been kissed before on stage and off it, but never like this. And never by Keel. The effect upon her was as unexpected as it was devastating, and Ros trembled under his hold.

'You're still cold.'

Keel mistook her trembling, and took the shawl from her arm and draped it back across her shoulders. Making sure she did not get a sore throat that would prevent her from singing for Milly? Silently reminding her that she was an employee at the Casa, and not a guest?

Depression descended upon Ros as she walked beside Keel back to the minibus. When he stopped at the exhibition hall and left her to collect his other passenger, she changed her seat to one further back in the bus, and left the seat beside Keel to be taken by the man who was joining them for the celebration party that evening.

Keel's eyes narrowed, spotting her move the instant he returned. She saw his face tighten, but he made no comment, and the other man got in beside him, unaware of the electric tension between his two companions.

Heavy tourist traffic on the road back made conversation spasmodic, and Ros was glad to leave what little there was to the newcomer. She tried unsuccessfully to stuff the shawl inside the carrier bag out of her sight, but the bag did not seem to have the capacity that its size promised, and the springy wool refused to stay folded, until with a shrug she gave up trying and returned the shawl to its former position over her arm.

As soon as the minibus stopped in front of the Casa, Una strolled to meet them, betraying the fact that she must have been watching out for their return. Her eyes winged straight to Ros's hair.

Too late, Ros remembered the carnation. She had meant to remove the flower during the journey, knowing that Una was bound to make capital of it. She berated herself for cowardice in pandering to the other girl's spite, but she felt wearily that Keel's presence in the house presented sufficient hazards after this morning's episode and, with the rest of the fortnight still to go, she did not want to add any more difficulties to them.

Una must be familiar with the gypsy's cry, 'A flower for the lady,' and would guess how she had acquired the carnation. The black eyes glittered as they roved insolently from the flower to the shawl, and from that to the bulky carrier bag in Ros's hand. The full lips sneered.

'I see you've had a good day's angling,' Una said.

Ros gave a gasp of anger, but before she could retort Keel rounded the front of the minibus and begged,

'Take care of Benito for me, Una, there's a love, while I go in and get changed. Give the man a drink. He must need one. It's been a sticky journey.'

He did not suggest that Ros might need a drink as well. The journey had been just as sticky for her, in more ways than one, she thought ruefully, and her throat felt parched, but presumably Keel considered that employees should fend for themselves.

Not that Ros wanted a drink from Una. Any

refreshment from that quarter would be mixed with malice, and taste accordingly. But the 'love' stung, emphasising the difference in their positions as nothing else could have done.

Una put her hand on Benito's arm and smiled up into the dark Spanish face, happy enough to be given the task of looking after a male guest, and Ros turned away and slipped unnoticed through the archway into the cool of the marble hall, suddenly longing for solitude. She had almost gained her room when she heard Keel's voice.

'Ros . . . Ros?'

She pretended not to hear him. It had taken him an unconscionable time to notice that she was not still with them, so whatever it was he wanted could not be of any great importance.

Ros tossed her purchases on to the bed and helped herself to a glass of iced orange juice from the fridge in her room, Milly's thoughtful provision for all her guests. She felt thankful that she could quench her thirst without recourse to an invitation from either Keel or Una.

A shower revived her, and she turned her attention to her purchases. The long cotton skirt would probably need to be pressed before she wore it, and there was less than an hour before dinner time.

She shook out the contents of the carrier bag on to the bed. Soft violet silk spilled from out of layers of tissue-paper wrappings. Ros stared at it disbelievingly. Without picking it up, she knew at once what it was.

The long violet evening dress.

The dress that Keel had said matched her eyes exactly. The one he had wanted her to buy, and she had returned to the rack because it bore no price tag.

Predictably, it still bore none. Ros investigated its folds with fingers that trembled with anger. Keel had done this. She had heard him talking to the assistant while she was in the cubicle trying on the rest of the garments.

Fury shook her at his high-handed action. How dared he presume to dictate what she should wear? How dared he spend her money for her? For that was what he had done. After what she had said in the store, he must know she would not accept the dress as a gift from Milly.

She would not wear it, Ros vowed.

She would go down to dinner as she had intended, dressed in the cotton skirt and top she had chosen for herself, and let Keel see what she thought of his dictatorial action.

The very next day she would return the dress to the store, if she had to walk every inch of the way into town to get there. Keel would not get away with dictating to her, she promised herself furiously.

A gentle tap sounded on her door, and she called, 'Come in.' It would be the maid, coming to see if she needed anything before dinner.

Quickly Ros hung the violet dress on the outside of the wardrobe, and shook out the long cotton skirt and top. They both looked crumpled from their journey, and the maid had come at just the right time to freshen them with an iron.

'My dear, it's perfect,' Milly enthused.

It was the artist, not the maid. Milly was resplendent; Ros scarcely recognised her as the vague, paint bespattered, untidy individual she had known until now. Her visitor's face broadened into a gamine grin.

'I like to startle my friends now and then,' she chuckled.

Ros felt herself go pink. 'I'm sorry. I didn't mean . . .'

'Of course you didn't. Blame my zany sense of humour. But I really came to see your dress, not to show off my own.' Milly gazed admiringly at the violet creation on the hanger. 'It's an inspiration, nothing less. Keel told me what a clever choice you'd made.'

It was Keel's choice, not her own, and he was using this method to foist it on to her in a way that he hoped would make her unable to refuse it.

How wrong he was, he had yet to find out, Ros fumed.

'You must wear it when I paint your portrait. We'll have the first sitting tomorrow morning, early, when the light's at its best.'

'Sit for you, in that dress?' Even though Keel was not in the room, Ros could feel the pressure of his indomitable will forcing her into submission.

'But of course. Nothing else will do. The dress is *you.*'

It was Keel. Pressure began to build up inside Ros to an unbearable degree that made her want to scream and throw things, preferably the dress at its domineering donor.

She grabbed up the cotton skirt. 'I thought this might . . .'

'It's very nice.' Milly gave the long cotton skirt

hardly a glance. 'It'll do for tomorrow, when Keel takes us all over to the island for a picnic. But tonight you must wear the violet dress so that I can watch you in it. It helps to watch a sitter wearing the clothes they're going to pose in. I like to watch gestures, and how the material falls with certain movements, and how it shades in different lights.'

Milly gave Ros a warm smile. 'It's so good of you to agree to sit for me. I'm sure it'll be my best portrait yet. There's an important exhibition of portraits to be held in New York at the end of the summer, and the canvas that's judged to be the best is allowed to be hung in the premier position in the gallery for a year. It's a very prestigious thing in the artistic world, and I'm human enough to covet it.' She gave Ros a look of appeal. 'All the works have to be new ones, but most of mine have been hung before, and I'd dearly love to exhibit. If you would only agree to stay on for an extra week or two, and I work very hard, I'm sure I could finish it in time to enter.'

It was impossible to refuse Milly, even if she could afford to. To do so would be to take more away from the artist than mere money. With a feeling of utter helplessness, Ros knew she must capitulate, and she loathed Keel for being instrumental in putting her in this position.

She would wear the dress this evening. But it would be for Milly, and not because Keel wanted her to, she told herself fiercely. And to pay for it, she would have to remain at the Casa for those extra weeks, whether she wanted to or not.

Emphatically, she did not. After her experience that

morning with Keel, her one desire was to leave the
Casa and its guests behind her, as far and as fast as
possible.

Contrarily, when Ros put on the long violet dress,
it restored her confidence. In spite of her determination not to look at herself, her eyes were drawn
irresistibly to her reflection in the long mirror, and
they widened at what they saw. The girl looking back
at her resembled a piece of exquisite porcelain.

The dress fitted as if it had been made for her. It
flowed over her slender body like a wing caressing
the softly rounded form of a bird, its delicate material
subtly outlining her limbs as she moved.

Her pupils, widened by the fading light, made two
matching pools of deep violet in the delicate frame of
her face, and, as a concession to Milly's celebration
evening, she had left her hair loose, allowing it to fall
freely in deep, shining waves across her shoulders.

At Milly's insistence, Ros wore a choker of pearls to
break up the deep neckline of the dress. They
gleamed with a delicate lustre against the soft
whiteness of her throat, and she slipped on a
matching bracelet to complete the set.

Milly had said with delightful frankness as she gave
them to Ros, 'They're not real; they're made on the
island. You can give them back to me after the
portrait's finished. But you must wear them. They're
just what the dress needs.'

It needed nothing more. The folds of the skirt
whispered softly against her feet, encased in silver
sandals which Milly had produced with a triumphant
flourish when she discovered that Ros took the same

size footwear as herself.

She would return these, too, afterwards. But, for now, Ros knew she looked her best, and the knowledge gave her the confidence she needed as she went downstairs to join the artist and her guests on the terrace.

Silence dropped on the gathering when she joined them. Taped music played on in a void of stilled conversation, and every eye turned to Ros as she paused for a moment in the wide doorway, before stepping on to the terrace.

She was aware of only three of the stares. Milly's eyes followed her, but Ros could discount the artist, whose look was friendly. Una's was quite the reverse.

As Ros appeared, a small hiss escaped the dark-haired girl, cutting across the silence like a sibilant exclamation mark, and the look on her face spoke louder than words. Ros turned her eyes away, and instinctively they sought Keel.

She knew he, too, was watching her. Among all the other eyes that rested on her, she could feel the power of Keel's tawny stare cutting through the others with the ease of a reaper cutting a swathe through standing corn. But if his expression was one of triumph, seeing her wearing the dress he had chosen for her, he must also read proud rejection of his victory in her look, because she was wearing the dress for Milly, and not for him.

Her glance met and locked with Keel's across the heads of the others, isolating them for a long, electric moment, and then the gong sounded, announcing dinner, and the spell, if such it was, was broken.

Suddenly everyone began to talk at once, too loudly, as if the passing current had momentarily touched them, too, and they felt, and were afraid of, its power.

Milly thrust aside her preoccupation during the meal and set herself out to be entertaining, confirming Keel's assertion that she could relax on occasion if she wanted to. Ros made herself respond, determined not to allow herself to be browbeaten by Keel or Una. She even put herself out to speak to Una, but the other girl responded with a blank stare, and Ros felt glad when Milly announced, during the barren minutes which inevitably follow a meal before other activities get under way, 'Ros is going to sing for us. Anything will do, my dear, so long as we can enjoy your lovely voice.'

'For goodness sake sing something a bit more up-to-date than those terrible oldies you raked up last night,' Una demanded rudely.

Ros kept her temper with an effort. She reminded herself tightly that she was employed to help Milly to entertain her guests, of whom Una was one, so she sang some of the songs that Una wanted, although they did not suit her voice, or her mood.

What was her mood?

It was becoming increasingly difficult to tell. Her feelings were more mixed than those of a teenager. The most recognisable was anger, and it did not help to realise that her anger was directed as much against herself as against Keel and Una, that she should be so weak as to allow either of them to disturb her normally serene composure.

She sang half a dozen songs, then Keel strode over to her with a cool drink, and ordered her abruptly, 'Have a rest while we dance.'

He went away again immediately and switched on a tape, as if he was bored with her singing and could not wait for her to finish so that he could do something more interesting, like dance with Una.

Ros sipped her drink and watched them together, and the fresh orange juice, that she had found so sweet and enjoyable until now, tasted bitter on her tongue, so that she left most of it untouched in the glass.

The dancing was a repeat of the previous evening, but it was too early yet for Ros to be able to slip away, and she resigned herself as best she could to enduring the blare of noise which seemed to have no impact upon the performers.

Even they tired eventually, however, and returned to their tables for a drink to refresh themselves. Across the blessed silence that ensued Keel called across to Ros, 'You can carry on singing now. Sing something to please Milly.'

Sing to while away the time for them while they recharged their batteries for another bout of dancing. Like a jester, called upon to amuse the assembled company at the click of a royal finger.

Ros felt the muscles of her throat begin to tighten with anger, but forced herself to relax. She had a purpose in singing, which was to rescue her pride by paying back every penny—or peseta; her lips curled—that her new clothes had cost, including the violet dress and the shawl, and whatever change was left over from the money Milly was to pay her would pay for the carnation as well.

So Ros raised her voice and sang again. She found it easier this time because she was singing the songs that Milly liked, which meant she herself liked them, too. It gave her a wider repertoire, enabling her to sing different songs from the ones she had used the evening before.

They were all love songs. Which of those that endured were not? The songs endured for longer than love itself, Ros thought cynically, as her tongue slipped almost without knowing it into the familiar verses of the last one.

'Will you dance with a stranger?'

Her audience listened in silence to the musical invitation. 'Will you dance with a stranger . . . if that stranger is me?'

The notes throbbed into the silence, and out of the corner of her eye Ros saw Keel move. He strode across to the tape recorder and began to sift through the tapes. Using his action as a silent signal to her that he had had enough, and wanted the dancing to begin again?

With a mental shrug Ros accepted the hint, and reached for her glass of orange juice. She had it raised half-way to her lips when her hand stilled. Keel slotted the tape into place but, instead of the raucous blare she expected from the loudspeakers, the music whispered a soft invitation.

'Will you dance with a stranger?'

It was like the echo of her own voice coming back to

her. At first Ros thought her imagination was playing tricks, but the tape continued to play, and Una's furious, 'You're blatant, aren't you?' was real enough, accusing her of directing her song specifically at Keel.

He was real. He shouldered his way through the people pairing off to dance, and made his way, not towards Una, but towards herself. Ros felt her pulse quicken as he approached.

With the swiftness of a striking snake Una uncoiled her sinuous body from off her chair and moved to intercept him, but a dancing couple blocked her way. Keel passed on and stopped in front of Ros, and asked her gravely, 'Will you dance with a stranger?'

He, too, thought her song had been an invitation, or why should he ask an employee to dance?

Ros burned with humiliation. When she sang, nothing had been further from her mind than to invite Keel to dance with her. In spite of Una's accusation, she would never be so blatant.

Would she?

The sudden doubt startled her. Had her tongue unconsciously chosen the song to transmit a message that her conscious mind would not acknowledge? If so, Keel had understood it, and responded.

He reached out and took Ros in his arms, and drew her with him towards the space on the terrace cleared for dancing. Ros stiffened.

'You're not a stranger. You said so yourself.'

She could not spurn him openly without causing comment, and she cursed her wayward tongue that had led her into this trap. Keel's arms clamped round her like a vice, blocking any hope of escape.

Fearful that he might pursue the subject, she sidetracked swiftly with, 'Why did you have this dress put in with my purchases? You saw me put it back on the rack.'

'It's perfect for you.'

'*I* decide what clothes are perfect for me. You have no right . . .'

'Milly gave me the right. She told me she wanted to paint you in something very special. The dress looks special, on you.'

Inferring that it was she who made the dress special, and not the other way round? The imp inside Ros began to purr, and angrily she slapped it into silence.

'I've got other clothes which are just as suitable.'

'They're locked in your suitcase, in Paris.'

'It should catch up with me in a day or two.'

'Milly can't wait a day or two. When she sets her mind on a new canvas, she has to start it right away, while the adrenalin's flowing. You don't have to pay for the dress yourself.'

Ros's chin came up proudly. 'I told you before . . .'

'You buy your own clothes,' he mimicked, mocking her pride. 'I know. But you could accept the dress as your fee for sitting for Milly, since she specially wants it.'

'What fee? Now you're being patronising.'

'On the contrary. If Milly engages someone to sit for her, she expects to pay a considerable fee for their services. If the portrait's commissioned, of course, the sitter does the paying.'

'Milly didn't engage me to sit for her.'

In fact, Milly had not engaged her at all. Lyn had thrust her willy-nilly into this situation, which had been out of her control right from the start, Ros thought bitterly. Not quite from the start. Rather, from the moment she had linked up with Keel.

'I'm not an artist's model.'

'You're a stubborn creature, with far too much stiff-necked pride,' he growled. 'If you don't want the dress after the portrait's finished, you can return it to Milly along with the gee-gaws she lent you to go with it.'

His contempt for her borrowed jewellery stung two angry spots of colour into Ros's cheeks.

'Because the pearls aren't real ones, it doesn't mean they're not beautiful.' Wealthy people were impossible, she fumed. They imagined that nothing had merit unless it cost the earth. Out loud she flashed, 'It isn't necessary to pay a fortune to get something beautiful. Quite cheap things can be lovely, too.'

'I agree,' he answered, and there was something in the deep timbre of his voice, and in the way he looked down into her face, that made Ros catch her breath. Keel's eyes must tell him she was beautiful. did he also regard her as being cheap?

Through a mist of anger she heard one of the guests cry, 'Let's all go down to the beach. It'll make a change from dancing.'

There was a general exodus from off the terrace and, grasping at the excuse, Ros said hastily, 'I'll go up and get my wrap. It's getting chilly.'

She would go to her room and remain there, and the others could have the beach to themselves and welcome. She was about to make her escape when Milly foiled her by insisting, 'You must come with us. It's lovely on the beach in the moonlight.'

'I'll follow you in a few minutes,' Ros capitulated reluctantly. The artist nodded, and turned to Una.

'Take my arm, my dear. I find the path to the beach a little rough.'

She held out her arm to the younger woman, and Una had no option but to take it, but she immediately reached out her other hand and grasped Keel's sleeve, demanding, 'Steer us. I'm as blind as a bat in the dark.'

They moved away with Walsh, and Ros went in search of her shawl, taking as long as she could to allow the others to get well away before she started after them. Milly walked slowly, and Ros felt she needed time on her own to straighten out her thoughts before she met up with Keel again.

He was becoming a threat to her peace of mind. His dictatorial ways repelled her, but some perverse chemistry in her make-up, that she could neither explain nor understand, drew her to him with a magnetic pull, and so far as she was concerned it was wholly unwelcome.

Before she met Keel, Ros had never doubted her ability to control her own life, even during her affair with Lomas. Now, less than forty-eight hours after meeting Keel, he had reduced her to a state where she was having difficulty in controlling her own thoughts, to an extent where her rebel tongue followed suit, and shamed her by calling him to dance.

Making her cheap in his eyes.

Nervous energy made Ros pace backwards and forwards across the bedroom carpet for a full ten minutes before she finally draped the despised shawl across her shoulders and made her way to the start of the track through the pinewoods.

The moonlight barely penetrated the trees, bright though it was, the close canopy overhead made an impenetrable umbrella, except now and then when the breeze parted the needles for a second or two and let in a brief chink of light. She would need to walk cautiously. Milly had said the path to the beach was rough, and the pale ribbon through the woods led into almost total blackness.

Ros gave a slight shiver, and instinctively pulled her shawl closer about her shoulders. Something dropped from above her on to the ground at her feet, and she started nervously. Her toe kicked the cause of her fright, and a large pine cone bounced along the path, making crisp little sounds on the tinder-dry needles.

A voice said, 'Be careful how you step. The tree roots can trip you.'

Ros froze, and her eyes dilated, trying to pierce the darkness in the direction of the voice.

'Did I startle you? I didn't mean to.' Keel unpeeled himself from against a precautionary stack of fire beaters and materialised out of the blackness.

'You're trembling. Did I frighten you so badly? I stayed behind to guide you to the beach.'

Keel was beginning to frighten her very badly indeed, but not because he had waited for her in the pinewood. Ros dredged her voice into use.

'I could have found the way by myself.' Ignoring his hand held out to guide her, she walked on, and was about to pass by him when she stumbled over one of the roots he had warned her against.

She fell into Keel's arms. Even as she went down, Ros thought, 'This is the sort of trick Una would use to make him put his arms round her.' And wondered if Keel would think she herself had stumbled with the same ulterior motive. Her pride withered under the contempt he must feel, even though she knew her fall was genuine.

Shaken as much by her conflicting thoughts as by the stumble, she trembled more violently still, and Keel drew her close against himself in order to steady her.

'Stand still for a few minutes until your eyes get adjusted to the light,' he said. 'You'll be able to see more clearly where you're going then.'

Ros felt she would give a good deal to be able to see more clearly where she was going, but not in the way Keel meant. Her eyes were adjusting to the stark whiteness of his shirt front close against her face. It cut a path through the blackness of his evening clothes, and nervously she tried to pull away from him.

'I'm fine now,' she lied.

'You're still shaking.' His arms tightened round her, resisting her move to break away. 'Wait until you steady down.'

How could she steady down while his arms were still round her? His one hand smoothed across the top of her hair, and his deep voice rumbled through his chest as his seeking fingers discovered, 'You're not wearing my carnation.'

His carnation.

As if, by giving it to her, he retained some right over the flower, and over its wearer. Ros bridled.

'The colour clashes with the dress.'

She refused to call it her dress, because she had not paid for it, and the sudden stiffening of his arms told her the omission had been noticed and understood.

Ros felt she needed her anger as an armour. Every tingling nerve of her was vividly aware of Keel, aware of subtle messages flowing from him that stirred her pulses to quickened life.

The wind parted the branches above them, and briefly the moonbeams illumined the sharp planes of his face, downturned over her own, before the branches surged together and brought the darkness back again. Her heart began to beat with a suffocating unevenness in time with her pulse, and she babbled urgently,

'Let's move on. Milly . . .'

'Milly won't need you.' He made no effort to move on. 'She's got Una with her, and Walsh.'

'She might want me to sing again.'

'So she might. And you do it beautifully.'

Keel's arms tightened, straining her to him, stilling her convulsive movement to break free, and his voice taunted her through the darkness.

'You sing of love, fair Rosalind. Is it just a song to

you, I wonder? Or do you know what love really is?'

And, bending his head lower still, he sent his lips to seek an answer for themselves.

CHAPTER FIVE

'DO YOU know what love really is?'

The question hammered in Ros's mind, tormenting her.

Keel's kiss tantalised her lips until they pursed under the pressure, giving him the response he was seeking with a will that defied her own. Triumphantly his mouth began to explore, and trailed ecstasy across her eyes and cheeks and hair, and she gave a tiny moan as his lips stroked along the slender column of her throat to where the choker of pearls rested in the delicate hollow at its base.

Artificial pearls.

Pearls that belonged to her world, but not to his. Arrogantly he had scorned their beauty because they were not real.

Just as his kiss was not real, because of the void that lay between their two worlds. Her beauty tempted him to lean across the chasm to pluck the flower on the other side that caught his passing glance, but, accustomed to the exotic hot-house blooms on his own side, he would tire soon enough of the simple loveliness he held in the circle of his arms, and toss it aside to return to the dark orchid that offered itself so freely for his gathering.

Ros began to struggle in Keel's arms.

'Let me go. Someone will come.'

'You're beautiful.' His voice was hoarse, and uncaring if anyone came.

In desperation Ros raised balled fists to hammer her message on his white shirt front. 'Loose me!'

Bitterly, she felt she was being used by Keel, who was rich and handsome and eligible, and who had only to lift a finger to have women to run to his side. So let him beckon the women of his own world, and leave her alone.

'Keel? Keel, where are you? Milly wants you.' Una's voice, a voice from his own world, calling him back. It came from the darkness of the pine plantation, where Una had earlier claimed she needed Keel's hand to guide her, but she seemed to have no difficulty now in making her way back to him.

'Keel, where are you?'

His arms slackened their grip on Ros. Grasping the opportunity, she wrenched herself free and was a yard away, smoothing her tumbled hair, when Keel answered, 'Over here. I'm waiting for Ros.'

Blaming her for the delay. Ros's fingers gripped convulsively on the silken strands and pulled, and the sharp pain steadied her sufficiently to meet Una with at least outward composure as the other girl came up to them, eyeing Ros suspiciously.

Walsh followed close on her heels and remarked amiably, 'Ah, there you are. You were so long, Milly wondered if you'd taken the wrong turning in the track.'

She had taken the wrong turning the morning she

started out on her journey to Majorca, Ros thought bitterly, but out loud she said, 'I tripped on a tree root, so I waited until my eyes got used to the darkness.'

Her eyes were staring at a darkness deeper than that of any pine wood, and she was only half aware of Walsh drawing her hand through his arm, and inviting her cheerfully, 'Hang on to me. I'll guide you. It's lighter on the beach.'

Silver sand gleamed softly in the moonlight, product of millions of tiny shells ground to powder by the remorseless action of the waves rolling shorewards in slow, heavy combers. Ros watched them roll, and felt an affinity with the hapless shells.

If Keel kissed her again with such compelling thoroughness, would she have the strength to withstand his onslaught, that left her feeling shaken still?

Out of the corner of her eye she saw him begin to walk towards her as she left Walsh and strolled slowly, on her own, along the edge of the water, and in self-defence she began to sing, using music as a shield to keep him away.

Her voice mingled with the soft drag of the waves on the sand. She saw Keel draw back in deference to her singing, and felt no sense of triumph at her victory; only a sense of irony that her song should be of love, while the singer walked alone at the edge of the moonlit sea.

'Do you know what love really is?'

Hours later Keel's voice returned to taunt Ros as

she tossed to and fro in the sleepless dark. Was what she had felt for Lomas real love? Or was it only a pallid reflection that was, she realised with a feeling of disbelief, already beginning to fade in the light of what had happened in the pine wood? If that was a reflection, how did one recognise the real thing?

Shadows bruised her eyes the next morning, evidence of her restless night, and Milly exclaimed when she appeared on the terrace at breakfast time, 'You look absolutely ethereal. Late nights suit you. Go and get changed right away; I must catch the look on canvas before it fades.'

Faded was how she felt this morning. Ros grimaced, but obediently she returned to her room and donned the violet dress, and the pearls and silver slippers of the night before.

After a brief mental struggle, she took the cashmere shawl along, too. She was not sure where Milly would want her to sit, and the morning wind was still cool, coming off the sea.

To her consternation, Keel and Una were both on the terrace when she returned, and she gritted her teeth as Una looked her up and down insolently, gave a tinkling laugh, and said, 'Have you been to bed in your clothes? How quaint.'

As a piece of friendly humour, it would not have rated very highly, but coming from Una it was calculated rudeness, and Ros restrained herself with an effort.

'Wander round the terrace,' Milly directed her. 'Pose here and there for me, so that I can decide on the best background.'

Under Una's sarcastic stare, it was almost impossible to carry out Milly's instructions in an unselfconscious manner, and Keel looking on made it infinitely worse.

Ros felt stiff, and wooden, and found it impossible to relax as she moved from place to place as she was bidden. Her nerves screwed into a tight ball in her stomach, tensing her all over, until Milly said smilingly, 'Relax, dear. I'm going to paint you, not eat you.'

Una's laugh shrilled out again, and Ros gave an irritable jerk with her head. Keel took the dark-haired girl by the arm and said,

'Let's go. We're in the way.'

'No. It amuses me to watch.'

Una remained where she was, indolently leaning against the balustrade, goading Ros to the point where she was about to make a sharp rejoinder, when Milly took a hand with unexpected authority.

'Run along, Una, there's a dear,' she said and, although her words were affectionate enough, her tone was unmistakably firm. 'You're distracting me and my model.'

Una shrugged. 'I mustn't distract your model from the work she's paid to do, must I?' Her high laugh echoed back mockingly as she went off with Keel, walking, Ros thought disgustedly, as close to him as a second skin.

They disappeared from sight among the pines, and she felt herself go limp. Milly advised, 'Stand at ease, while I sort out my paints and things.'

Thankful for the respite, Ros sank on to the top terrace step, and leaned her back against a stone pillar. She did not need the shawl after all. The terrace was sheltered from the wind by the pines, and she allowed the delicately coloured cashmere to trail down the steps at her feet.

Milly seemed to be a long time fussing with her painting materials, and Ros leaned her head back against the pillar, and let her thoughts drift. Her eyes followed the violet heads of wisteria, swinging lazily in the breeze. Whenever I see the colour violet, it'll remind me of Keel, she thought. She would avoid the colour in future, she planned. But how, when her own eyes would reflect it every time she looked in the mirror?

She turned her head restlessly, as if to avoid the reflection now, and Milly urged her instantly, 'Don't move. Your pose is perfect, just as you are.'

It was not a deliberate pose. Lost in her own reflections, Ros had not noticed the artist was already busy at her easel, painting with speed and concentration. She resumed her former stance, watching the wisteria blow in the breeze, and tried ineffectually to empty her mind of Keel.

An impossible task, she discovered to her chagrin, when it persisted in wondering where Keel—and Una—were, and what they were doing. Were they wandering together in the pinewood? And if so, was Keel . . .

Ros stopped her thoughts sharply, but the effort must have caused her to move again, because Milly said solicitously, 'Are you getting stiff? We'll finish now, and have another session tomorrow morning at the same time.'

'I'm not stiff, really, if you want to carry on.'

'No, I'm going out with Walsh this morning, into town. Which reminds me, I want you to do something for me while I'm away.'

'What is it?' Ros got up and strolled towards the easel. 'May I see?'

'No.' The artist shook her head. 'I never show my canvases until they're complete. You shall come to the exhibition and see the portrait there as it should be seen, framed, and properly hung.'

'That would be lovely,' Ros replied, and knew she lied because, once she left the Casa, nothing would induce her to face the possibility of meeting Keel again. To divert Milly from the subject, she reminded her, 'You wanted me to do something for you.'

'Yes.' Briefly a frown crossed the artist's forehead. 'It's about the picnic supper on the island this evening. I'd like you to go over the menu with Maria. She's an excellent housekeeper, but she likes to have my support for her choice of menu when I'm entertaining, particularly when there's a young crowd among the guests. She hasn't been with me long enough to feel entirely confident that our tastes coincide.'

By a young crowd, she must mean Una's crowd.

It was delicately put, but there was no mistaking the inference, and Ros wondered why the frown. Maria's menus had been beyond criticism, since she had been at the Casa, so what could a young crowd possibly want more than Maria was likely to provide?

'I'll do what I can,' Ros agreed, and after waving Milly and Walsh off she went indoors in search of the housekeeper. Maria was in the breakfast room, seated at a table beside the open french windows, and Una was with her.

The housekeeper looked flustered, and Ros was about to back away without disturbing them when Maria caught sight of her and called out, 'Miss Morland, please, a minute?'

'This has got nothing to do with her,' Una snapped as Ros walked into the room, but, seeing what she obviously hoped was reinforcement arriving, Maria plucked up the courage to differ.

'Miss Fisher said Miss Morland was to go through the menu with me, while she was in town, Miss Una.'

'I'm quite capable of deciding what we want for the picnic.'

The housekeeper's face tightened, and Ros intervened. 'Could I see the menu, Maria?'

She held out her hand for the piece of paper that the housekeeper was twisting into a creased spill between angry fingers. Ros straightened it out and scanned the neat writing.

'Is all this local produce?' At the housekeeper's nod she went on encouragingly, 'It looks delicious. Lobster salad, buttered artichokes, fresh strawberries, mmm . . . And the local wine is very good. I had some with my lunch yesterday.'

'Any plonk would taste good to someone not used to wine,' Una snapped.

Ros gave her a straight look. 'Keel chose the wine.'

Una went scarlet, but she fought back. 'I want champagne, and those big, imported strawberries. I saw some in town the other day.'

'Miss Morland?' The housekeeper turned harassed eyes on Ros.

'The local wine is adequate for a beach picnic, and imported strawberries are an unwarranted extravagance when Milly grows her own here at the Casa.'

'This is a Casa Mimosa picnic, not the sort of beefburger and chips takeaway you're probably used to.'

'It isn't a Ladies' Day picnic at Royal Ascot, either.' Ros returned the menu to Maria and said firmly, 'The wine and food you've chosen will do beautifully, Maria.'

Una's eyes flashed. 'How dare you override me? A mere outsider . . .'

'I dare because Milly asked me to agree the picnic menu with Maria.' Privately Ros thought, I know now why Milly frowned, but out loud she said sweetly, 'Of course there's nothing to stop you from treating everyone to champagne at your own expense, if you want to.'

For a fraught moment she thought Una would strike her. The other girl's face went scarlet, and then white, and she had difficulty in summoning her voice. At last she managed a strangled, 'I've changed my mind. We won't have a picnic after all. We'll have a barbecue instead.'

'But Miss Una, the food's already prepared.'

'I said a barbecue. A *barbecue*, do you understand? Not a picnic.'

'The island's covered in pine woods, miss, and they're tinder dry. The risk of fire . . .'

'I don't care about the risk! I don't care about the

food!'

Una was getting shrill, and Ros decided her impossible behaviour had gone far enough. She remembered the stand of fire beaters against which Keel had leaned the night before; they were not placed there for decoration.

'I care,' she broke in firmly. 'If you won't listen to common sense, somebody must make you.'

'Who? You?' Una sneered.

'No, Keel.' Ros stepped to the window and called out sharply, 'Keel, can you spare a minute please?'

She had spied him a second or two earlier, walking in the garden beyond the windows. Perhaps waiting for Una?

She would have preferred to handle the matter herself, but the prospect of being thwarted seemed to have driven Una into a frenzy, and since Keel seemed to regard it as his divine right to take charge of everything and everybody, let him take charge of this, she thought unrepentantly.

She waited tensely as he strode through the french windows to join them, and Una spun to meet him.

'Keel, I want . . .'

'Mr Hennessy, Miss Fisher told me to . . .'

'One at a time.' Keel raised an authoritative hand which silenced both Una and Maria, and turned to the housekeeper. 'Maria first,' he said, courteously deferring to her age, regardless of her position in the household.

Una pouted, but a look from Keel dissuaded her from speech, and Maria complained, 'I've got all the food prepared for the picnic, and Miss Una's changed her mind and wants a barbecue instead.'

'It isn't on, love.' Keel tucked Una's hand through his arm and said mildly, 'You must have forgotten. The pine woods come right down to the shore on the island. One spark from a barbecue would be enough to set the woods alight in this heat. We'll have your barbecue another time, somewhere safer.'

He spoke as he would to a fractious child, which was exactly how Una had behaved, Ros thought waspishly. Love was said to be blind. Perhaps that was what afflicted Keel, or why else would he put up with the girl's outrageous behaviour? She watched tight-lipped as Keel coaxed Una away with, 'Come and look at the *Sea Spray*. Jean-Jacques brought her in this morning. She's just been refitted.'

He turned as they reached the french windows together, and spoke to Ros for the first time. 'By the way, your case has come on the yacht. I've had it sent up to your room.'

Ros's anger against Keel grew as she took her clothes out of her case and put them on to hangers. He must have left instructions for Jean-Jacques to pick up their cases from the Cher, and bring them along when he sailed the yacht round the coast to Majorca. He must have known it would arrive today, which meant that the major part of the shopping she had done yesterday had been totally unnecessary, including the long violet evening dress. The arrival of her suitcase made it not so much a dress as a manifestation of Keel's will imposed upon her own.

And now she had worn the dress to pose for Milly,

she would have to go on wearing it until the portrait
was finished.

Ros's victory over Una paled in comparison, and
spoiled her appetite for the dainty lunch which Maria
sent out to her on the terrace, making the offering
especially tempting as a silent thank-you for Ros's
support that morning.

She ate alone.

The guests had all disappeared, and presumably
Keel and Una were with them. Perhaps they were on
the *Sea Spray*, heading out across the millpond water
towards one of the many secluded coves that bit deep
into the island's coastline. Ros visualised the yacht
anchored in idyllic surroundings, its passengers
lazily sunbathing, or disporting themselves in the
water.

She gave an unconscious sigh. She loved
swimming and, in spite of her aversion to boats, the
hot sunshine made the water attractive, but she
supposed with a shrug that Keel did not consider her
eligible to join the party.

Restlessly she turned her attention to clothes for
the picnic that evening. However much it went
against their grain, Keel and Una would not be able to
exclude her from that. Milly had already intimated
that she wanted Ros to go along, and had even
suggested the long cotton skirt as suitable wear.

Ros eyed it discontentedly. She had taken an
irrational dislike to the beautifully cut garment
because of its association with the shopping trip with
Keel, and with a spurt of rebellion she tossed it aside
in favour of a pair of vividly patterned coolie-style

cotton trousers with a matching top, which would give her more freedom of movement for a beach picnic than the slenderly cut cotton skirt.

Would they swim before the meal? She did not know, but just in case she slipped into a fuchsia-coloured bikini and top underneath the trousers, and went down to the terrace at the appointed time to meet the others.

There was no one there. They had gone without her, after all.

Fury boiled in Ros, misting her vision, so that she did not immediately see the tall man who strolled across to her and enquired politely,

'Miss Morland?'

Ros nodded dumbly, and he went on, 'I'm Jean-Jacques. I skipper the *Sea Spray* for Mr Hennessy. He's taken all the others across to the island, and I've come back to collect you and Miss Fisher and Mr Craythorne. And the food, of course,' he smiled.

Ros found her voice. 'Do you want me to help carry baskets and things?'

'No. Maria sent the servants on ahead, to load the cool boxes into the galley.'

It was a small sop to her pride that she was not included among their number, and when Milly called out gaily, 'You two young people walk on. Walsh and I will follow at our own pace and meet you at the landing-stage,' Ros went with the burly skipper readily enough.

Unsure what to talk about, she chose the topic most likely to interest her companion.

'I understand the *Sea Spray's* just had a refit?'

'Yes. We tangled with some pretty heavy debris in the water a month or two ago, and the hull got damaged. Keel had the yacht taken into dry dock, and the whole thing refitted, and the engine overhauled while they were about it. He wants the vessel ready to take Miss Fisher to New York for her exhibition later this year. She hates flying, and she doesn't like the crowds on the transatlantic liners.'

Keel could be oddly sensitive to the needs of people in his own circle, when he chose, Ros reflected. Memory of his gentleness as he washed her face, and lifted her on to the *Sea Spray's* bunk, and tucked blankets round her, rebuked her for limiting the scope of his kindness, but she thrust it aside and forced herself to concentrate on what Jean-Jacques was saying as he resumed, 'We were lucky to get the refit done so quickly. It only needed the sea trials to throw up one snag, and it would have put us back another week or two.'

A thought crossed Ros's mind. 'When did you hold the sea trials?'

'Early yesterday. As soon as I got the OK, I telephoned a message through to the Casa, grabbed your luggage from the Cher, and kept going until I got here.'

Ros nodded abstractedly.

If Keel had not known until the last minute when the *Sea Spray* would be released, he could not have predicted when their luggage would arrive, either. Which meant that, at the time of their shopping trip, he must have thought her purchases were necessary.

Suddenly she wished she had put on the long cotton

skirt for the picnic after all, instead of her present outfit, but it was too late now to go back to her room and change.

In spite of their slower pace, Milly and Walsh were not long behind them and once on board, Ros remained with them on deck, leaning on the rail as Jean-Jacques took the yacht at an easy pace across the placid water.

The crossing took about half an hour, and as they approached the island Keel swam out to meet the boat. His strong arms cleaved the water, sending lines of tiny drops like diamonds dripping in the sun, and he raised a hand in greeting as he closed in on the yacht.

Milly and Walsh waved gaily back, but Ros kept her arms glued to the rail, and she froze, immobile, as Keel trod water below them, and tipped his head back to look up straight into her face.

His eyes narrowed against the sun, and although he could have been looking at either Milly or Walsh, leaning on the rail beside her, Ros knew he was not. His stare pierced through her, pinning her feet to the deck.

'Come and join me,' he called up to her.

Ros hesitated, and Milly enquired, 'Have you brought a costume?'

'I've got it on.'

A second later Ros could have bitten her tongue. She had come hoping to swim, but with all the guests together in the water, not with Keel alone. 'Later, perhaps,' she hedged.

'There's no need to be shy,' Milly smiled. 'Everyone will be in bikinis, if they're not already. I'll take your trousers and top ashore with me.'

A single word from the water below taunted Ros's hesitation.

'Scared?'

It sped upwards like an arrow, barbed and scornful, and Ros winced as it struck home.

Was she scared? Keel was still there, looking up at her, waiting for her answer.

His lips did not move, but the challenge was writ large on his face, and it was enough. Impulsively Ros stripped off her slacks and top, and shook her hair free from its restraining comb.

'Stay clear. I'm coming in,' she called, and dived.

She surfaced to find Keel beside her. He trod water, waiting for her to come up, and his eyes laughed into hers as she shook her face free of water, and stroked her saturated hair clear of her eyes.

His probed deep, penetrating her clear violet stare, and Ros said quickly, defensively, 'They're real. The colour doesn't run.'

Keel laughed. Strong white teeth slashed sun-bronzed skin, and his eyes borrowed the dancing glints from the water. 'I wasn't looking at your eyelashes.'

'Then what . . .'

Suddenly she did not want to know the answer. She backed water away from him, but he reached out a long arm and towed her back easily, holding her to face him.

'You look like a mermaid with your hair floating in the water,' he told her.

He ran exploring fingers through the floating gold strands, and the sensuous stroking motion sent a premonitory quiver through Ros. She was out of her depth with Keel. She floated easily enough in the clear Mediterranean blue, and drowned in the fathomless peat pools of his eyes.

Desperately she tried to tear her own away, but they were locked with a key she was unable to turn. In the warm blue water, with the sun beating down on her head, and already beginning to dry out the short soft tendrils around her temples, Ros shivered again.

'Your hair's like silk.' Keel's fingers tangled with the gold strands, and his touch sent shockwaves pulsing through Ros, electrifying the water round them.

'Do you sit on a rock in the moonlight and comb it, and sing siren songs to lure men to their doom?'

He lured Ros with stroking hands and smiling lips, and eyes that challenged her to follow him into waters in which she would not be able to keep afloat. If she took up the challenge, and dared to follow, the doom would be her own, not his.

With a quick wriggle she broke free from his hold.

'My eyes are the wrong colour. A mermaid's eyes are green,' she flashed, and dived.

Her hair streamed out behind her as she went down, down, into the mysterious green depths, surprising a shoal of tiny fish that dashed away in rainbow-hued panic.

She did not need to see the long, slim brown form behind her to know that Keel was following. The water carried the all-too-familiar message of his vibrations to her as she swam, and when pale sand rippled underneath her, and she felt her breath beginning to give out, he was beside her.

His hand reached out and found her fingers, and he turned her upwards with him through the water. It was like a dream dance, Ros thought wonderingly, as they rose together through the silent depths, joined in a close embrace. Keel's hands released her fingers, and his arms came right round her, and the pressure of his lips over her mouth locked in the last vestige of her pent-up breath.

They surfaced and broke apart, and gulped in lungfuls of clear, sweet air. Ros wondered why it should seem so strangely unsatisfying as it flowed across her abandoned lips, stale as nectar with all the sweetness removed.

With one accord they turned towards the shore, and her eyes picked out a lone figure standing at the water's edge, black-haired, and bright-bikinied. Keel must have spotted it, too, because he quickened his pace and headed towards it purposefully, beckoned, Ros told herself cynically, by his own world.

He made no attempt to slow down to allow Ros to keep up with him, and she was left behind, feeling thankful that only the green waters of the bay knew the secret of their kiss.

Keel strode dripping up the sloping beach to join Una, and called out, 'Why didn't you come along? The water's lovely.'

'Someone has to supervise the picnic.'

'The servants are quite capable. They're used to

organising beach picnics. And if they need guidance, Milly's there.'

'Milly!' Una snorted. 'She's so obsessed with Walsh, it isn't true. I don't understand what she sees in the man. He's ordinary to the point of distraction.'

'I like him. You're not looking at him through Milly's eyes, so you don't see his good points.'

'I can hardly see anything through my own. They're full of sand. Every time there's a puff of wind, this fine stuff drifts everywhere. I wish we hadn't come.'

Una kicked discontentedly at the sand, and sent showers of it on the breeze straight in Ros's direction.

She dodged swiftly, averting her face to avoid the stinging invasion, and felt an angry urge to slap the other girl. She could not prove that Una's action was deliberate, but at best it was a thoughtless thing to do to make the fine gritty particles airborne, particularly as Una had already complained of getting them in her own eyes.

Unless she was just saying that to try to get Keel to investigate her eyes to remove the grit? If so, Keel ignored her pointer and asked, 'Have you been sail-boarding?'

'No. I was waiting for you. Some of the others have got them out.'

'There aren't many on the water.' He cast a look at the bright sails, flitting like a flock of gaudy butterflies across the bay.

Una's lips curled. 'Some of them have never seen a sailboard before, let alone used one. There was no need to bring so many.'

'Why don't you teach them, so that they can share in the fun? Most of them are your guests.'

Was there just a hint of asperity in the normally mild tone Keel used towards Una? Ros wondered, and then decided she must be mistaken, because it was gone when he turned towards herself and asked, 'Have you ever used a sailboard, Ros?'

'No. It's something I've never tried.'

'I'll teach you,' Keel offered unexpectedly, and Una flashed him an angry look.

'It's a pity you don't take your own advice, and teach the *guests*,' she snapped, and Ros thought ruefully, that's put me in my place.

A gap in a group of palm trees revealed another small bay, with several sailboards lying unused on the sand, and a group of people lying indolently beside them, soaking up the sun. Una stalked away to join them, but instead of following her, Keel lifted the nearest sail and said, 'Would you like to try?'

It was an opportunity Ros could not miss. The sun and the sand and the shining sea beckoned her irresistibly to abandon her vow to keep the peace at all costs. It was a day made for fun, and she wanted to enjoy it to the full. Una could not be in a worse mood than she was now, and Ros turned her back on the other girl and accepted impulsively.

'I'd love to. Is the sail very heavy?'

'Not if you lift it correctly. Lean away as you pull it towards you. Your body will balance the board, and your own weight will help you to pull up the sail.'

Keel's lean brown fingers curled round the rope in a confident grip as he pulled it towards him, leaning outwards from it so that his body described a perfect arc opposite the rising sail.

Ros watched fascinated, her eyes on Keel rather than on the sailboard. He would make a wonderful painting, she thought, and wished she had Milly's skill with the brush. Against the backdrop of the bright sky and the dazzling sand, Keel's gold swimming trunks, a paler gold than his eyes, stood out in clear definition, complementing the deep, even tan of his athletic frame.

The multi-coloured sail came aloft with deceptive ease under his skilled manipulaton, and a small round of applause burst out and brought Ros back to earth with the realisation that they had collected an audience.

'Now you come and try,' Keel invited Ros, and, to the others, 'Get yourself a sailboard each, and have a go. You'll soon get the hang of it. If you get into difficulties, call Una or me, and we'll put you right.'

'I didn't come on a picnic to set up a sailing school,' Una muttered sulkily, but Keel ignored her, and concentrated instead on helping Ros.

His hands over her own on the rope lent them a magic skill, and all too soon it seemed to Ros she had mastered the art of raising the sail.

'That's good. That's fine. You're very quick to learn,' Keel praised.

Ros felt a glow of pride at his praise, and oddly bereft when he left her to rescue the others who were getting tangled in ropes and sails. Shouts of laughter rose from the erstwhile bored sunbathers, and it was a merry flotilla that set sail together a short time later.

It was much more difficult to cope with the sail on the water. The board rocked underneath Ros in a balance destroying manner, and the breeze puffed out the canvas, making it pull on her arms. The sudden tug pulled her body off balance, and the sailboard lurched alarmingly. The other learners were all experiencing similar difficulties, and several sails dropped ignominiously into the sea, tipping the would-be sailboarders to join them.

With a mighty heave of her straining muscles, Ros managed to right her own sail, and thrilled to the sensation as the board skimmed across the surface of the water, graceful as a skater on ice.

Another board skimmed along behind her, rapidly overtaking her. She turned her head, thinking it might be Keel, and saw that it was Una. The girl was cutting a path diagonally across the front of Ros's sailboard and, at the speed she was travelling, if she did not turn, they could not help but collide.

Ros raised her voice and shouted, 'Look out!'

Una ignored her, and came straight on, and Ros wrestled desperately with her sail, trying to turn her craft. Keel had demonstrated how to do it, but what had seemed a simple manoeuvre on shore seemed incredibly difficult on the unstable seaborne board.

'Look out!'

Una must have heard her. Ros saw the girl look round, and her face was hard and set as she came straight on. A crash was inevitable. Una's board struck Ros's craft a glancing blow, but immediately the other girl did something clever with her sail, and veered away, her balance unimpaired.

If she had done the same thing only seconds earlier they would have missed each other, which told its own story to Ros, who seethed impotently as Una's jeering laugh echoed across the water as she sped away and left Ros to her fate.

It was swift, and inevitable. The wildly bucking board tipped, the sail sank to rest on the water, and for the second time that afternoon Ros found herself having an unexpected dip.

It would have happened anyway, she told herself philosophically. By now, all the novices were in the same plight, and trying with varying degrees of success to raise their sails upright again.

Ros tried to raise her own, but the wet canvas was beyond her strength, and she began to swim ashore, towing her craft behind her. By now, Una was a considerable distance out in the bay, and Ros watched with narrowed eyes as another craft skimmed in the girl's wake. The gold swimming trunks of its rider told her it must be Keel.

If he was not careful, he would do exactly the same and collide with Una's sailboard, she realised, surprised, and trod water to watch the two. For someone as strong as Keel, it should have been easy for him to turn his craft but, like Una, he made no apparent attempt to do so.

Perhaps it was an accepted part of the sport, to crash one another's craft? Ros cast puzzled eyes at the other sailboarders, but she could see no evidence of such childish horseplay among them.

Una's shrill shout, 'Look out!' carried clearly to her across the water, echoing her own urgent warning, and then the two craft met, and in seconds Una, too, was floundering in the water beside her capsised sail.

Ros could not repress a grin as she returned to the task of towing her own craft back to the beach. She should have felt ashamed, but did not, as her parted lips let out a satisfied murmur, *'Touché!*

CHAPTER SIX

UNA'S temper was not improved when she came ashore.

Keel did not leave her to her fate, as Ros had been left when her craft founded. Immediately Una's sail touched the water, he dived from his own board to help her to right it, and as soon as she was aloft, he righted his own and they rode ashore in tandem.

Ros's pride was hurt at the contrast between Keel's treatment of Una and that of herself, however much she tried to ignore it; it took the shine from the sea, and the savour from the tempting picnic fare, which she guessed shrewdly was spoiled for most of the guests anyway by Una's behaviour.

The dark-haired girl snapped at the servants, criticised the food and drink, particularly the wine and the strawberries, and sulkily refused to join in the singing that broke out spontaneously after the meal was over. Voices rang out gaily, with Ros leading the songs, until Una brought all to an end by contemptuously comparing it to a girl guides' camp-fire sing-song.

The girl really was a spoiled brat, Ros thought disgustedly, and wondered if the discipline of having to work for her living might have improved the badly behaved sophisticate, whose background ensured she did not need to work.

After one particularly petulant outburst, even the tolerant Milly was driven to enquire, 'Have you got a headache, dear? Perhaps you've been in the sun too much. Come back home on the first trip across, with Walsh and me. We're going soon, although of course, you young ones can stay on for as long as you please.'

'I don't know why I came in the first place. There's nothing to do on the island, and it's dead boring.' Una turned to Keel and demanded, 'Take me for a run on the *Sea Spray* to make up. Show me what she's capable of since she's been refitted. It's ages since we've been on a long trip in her.'

The black sloe eyes slid across to Ros as she spoke, and Ros lifted her shoulders in the merest hint of a shrug that said it was no business of hers who Keel took on the *Sea Spray*, or for how long a voyage.

Instead of pandering to her, to Ros's surprise Keel replied evenly, 'You mustn't desert your guests,' and continued his conversation with those nearest to him. With an exclamation of temper Una tossed away her half-finished cigarette, and flounced off after Milly and Walsh towards the yacht.

Inevitably the unpleasant contretemps broke up the party, and the guests began to drift after their hostess. Ros hesitated, uncertain what she ought to do. Should she go along with Milly and Walsh? But that would mean her also going along with Una, and she drew back.

The yacht could not accommodate them all comfortably on one journey, and she had come out on the second trip across, so presumably she would be expected to return likewise, with the servants. Her lips twisted at the distinction as Keel intervened and made her decision for her with his instruction to Jean-Jacques,

'Take them across if they want to go back to the Casa, and then come back for us. In the meantime, we'll get the sailboards stacked ready for stowing.'

Ros assumed he meant himself, and one of the menservants, and felt a thrill of resentment when he turned to her and said, 'I'll show you how to deal with the sails.'

It erupted in her snapped reply, 'I'm employed to help Milly, not as a labourer.' How dare Keel use her as a jack-of-all-trades?

She was in no way mollified when he retorted, 'It's no use learning how to ride a sailboard, if you don't know how to cope with it on shore.'

'Una didn't stay behind to help.'

It was out before she could stop it. Ros squirmed as Keel's steely look raked her face, and she had difficulty in schooling her expression to resist it when he said, in an odd voice that gave his words a less than obvious meaning, 'Una never helps.'

Now she had gone this far, there was no point in holding back, and Ros let her resentment show.

'Her behaviour's impossible. Why do you allow it?' He controlled everybody else. Why could he not control Una?

'I have my reasons, and they're nothing to do with you.'

Nothing to do with an employee, he meant. Keel's

closed expression made his meaning clear enough, and he brought an end to the subject with a reiterated, 'I'll show you how to deal with the sails.'

'Get one of the menservants to do it,' Ros flared and, turning her back on him, she stalked away to the landing-stage. She was up the gangplank and on to the *Sea Spray's* deck almost before Jean-Jacques had had time to dock it properly.

She moved to stand against the furthest rail, ignoring Keel when he came on board with the menservants. Instead of moving forward to the wheelhouse to take the yacht out again, as she expected him to do, Keel left the task to the Frenchman, and came to stand beside Ros.

His nearness was disturbing. And unnecessary. There was a lot of rail for him to lean on without crowding her; he was so close that, when he leaned forward to watch the wake of the vessel begin to form behind them, his arm, lean and brown and tightly muscled, brushed against her own.

Ros jerked her arm away, and instantly Keel looked up and across at her, his eyes narrowing in the sun. Ros quickly turned her face away and looked pointedly back at the island.

It was then that she saw the smoke.

'Keel, look.' She pointed urgently, her temper forgotten in this new emergency. 'There's a fire on the island.'

Keel straightened swiftly and stared for a taut second. 'You mean, the island's on fire,' he ejaculated, and raised his voice to a shout. 'Jean-Jacques, put the *Sea Spray* about. Get a move on, man! We might be just in time.'

A tongue of flame underlined the urgency of his order. It flickered through the tinder-dry pine needles, and the acid smell of burning wafted to their nostrils on the breeze as the skipper swung the yacht over and made ful speed ahead, back towards the shore.

Straining her eyes towards it, Ros thought, 'Una's cigarette end . . .'

She did not voice her thought to Keel. What was the point? He would probably think she was trying to cause mischief if she did, and Keel had eyes of his own if he wished to use them, even if they were blind to Una's faults.

The conflagration was spreading, driven by the brisk breeze and fuelled by the abundant dry debris on the floor of the plantation.

'Pull into the bay,' Keel called to the skipper. 'I'll swim ashore. It'll be quicker than waiting until you've shunted into the landing-stage.' He turned to Ros and ordered her brusquely, 'Stay on board where you'll be safe.'

'If you're going ashore, I'm coming with you.' Ros did not pause to consider what impulse made her determined to accompany him, only that she knew she must.

'You're crazy. Your cotton trousers and top are as thin as paper. They'll catch alight at the first spark.'

'Not if they're wet, they won't.'

Adroitly Ros dodged Keel's detaining hand. With a gesture of defiance she ignored his angry shout, 'Ros, come back,' and scrambled over the rail and dived cleanly into the water.

She was glad she had not kicked off her sandshoes. Even through the sturdy rubber soles she could feel the heat of the ashes threaten her feet as she ran ashore.

Keel glanced down at them once and, seeing they were well protected, he headed towards a stack of besoms waiting in readiness for just such an emergency. Grabbing two, he tossed one to Ros, tacitly accepting her help, and side by side they began to beat frantically at the spreading flames that were beginning to roar hungrily, but had not as yet, Ros saw thankfully, infiltrated very far into the trees.

Perspiration poured down her face as she worked, joining the drips from her soaking hair. Her cotton trousers and top clung wetly to her body in a clammy embrace, outlining her perfect figure as she joined with Keel to fight the rapidly growing inferno.

She could see his face, grim and set, as he flailed at the flames beside her. The fire was getting out of hand. No sooner was one patch extinguished than another started somewhere else, and despairingly Ros felt her strength begin to flag.

The heat grew more intense, and the besom became heavier by the minute as she wielded it with straining arms, flogging out the flames. She looked across at Keel's face, streaked black with ash and soot and sweat, and knew her own must look the same.

'Ros, look out!'

Keel leapt towards her as a loud crack sounded from immediately above her head, and a large pine branch, burning like a torch, crashed down beside her. If it had not been for Keel, it would have landed right on top of her, she saw, shaken.

With one arm he hooked her clear, and with the other he gave a mighty swing at the branch and pushed it away from her. Even so she felt the heat from the flames rake her hair as it fell, and knew that if it, too, had not been wet from the sea, it would have set alight.

Soon, the whole island would become one huge torch.

'Over here,' Keel shouted. She looked round at him dazedly and realised he was shouting to someone over her head. She turned, and saw the menservants and Jean-Jacques dragging something long and heavy and bright scarlet up the beach towards them.

The yacht's skipper lifted one of the fire extinguishers in his arms, and a jet of foam sprayed the spot where the fire was at its height.

In the space of minutes, that seemed like hours to Ros, it was all over. The fire was reduced to smoking debris, and that, too, was being rapidly killed as the men formed a chain across the beach and passed buckets of water to thoroughly soak the whole area, until Keel was satisfied that there was no risk of it starting over again.

'That could have been nasty,' Jean-Jacques understated, as they stood gazing at the blackened patch.

Keel nodded. 'Another few minutes, and it would have been too late for us to be able to contain it.'

He wiped a weary hand across his smoke-blackened forehead, and Ros's eyes widened as they lighted on the long scorch weal on his skin.

'Your arm!' she exclaimed. 'You're burned.'

Impulsively she caught his hand and turned his arm towards her, and a gasp escaped her lips as she saw the rapidly forming blister run almost from elbow to wrist. 'The branch must have been red hot when it fell.'

Keel had burned himself in order to save the branch from falling on her.

A sudden lump choked Ros's throat. She excused it as a natural reaction to tiredness and fright, and swallowed it down, and said with a briskness that denied a wobbly feeling inside her, 'You must have your arm attended to right away.' There was a comprehensive first-aid kit on board the *Sea Spray*. She had seen it in the galley when she first went down there to drink Ella's tea, it seemed like a lifetime ago.

'I'll see to it when we get back to the Casa.'

'Burns need attention immediately, because of the risk of infection.' Confidence gained from experience helping out in her father's surgery steadied her voice, and she turned to Jean-Jacques. 'Is anyone else hurt?'

One of the menservants had a superficial burn. The *Sea Spray*'s skipper added his weight to Ros's advice. 'Ros is talking sense, Keel. Burns need cleaning and dressing quickly.'

'First of all, signal back to the Casa to let them know we're all safe,' Keel instructed. 'They'll have seen the smoke from the mainland, and I don't want Milly to be frightened.'

He said nothing about the possibility of Una being

frightened. Perhaps he knew her well enough to realise that she would not be overly concerned about anyone else's safety but her own.

The signalling done, Keel insisted that Ros dress the manservant's burn first, then sent him off to the galley with the others with instructions to Jean-Jacques to give them each a tot of rum and have one himself, before he submitted his own arm for attention.

Ros cleaned the badly scorched skin, and felt sick at the pain she knew she must be inflicting. Burns were the cruellest of wounds, and she said with a catch in her voice she could not control, 'I'm trying not to hurt you too much.'

If it had not been for Keel, she would be feeling the same, or worse, pain now.

'Go ahead, get it done,' he told her curtly.

His face was expressionless, reflecting none of the agony she knew he must feel each time she touched his arm.

He was hard. As hard with himself as he was with others, she thought with a sudden spurt of anger. And yet not hard all the way through, because he was considerate of Milly's peace of mind, sufficient to send her a signal that they were safe, in order to prevent her from worrying.

Ros bent her head over her task, conscious that Keel's eyes were following her every movement. Meticulously she cleaned the burn, and then carefully covered it with a sterile dressing and began to bandage with a fierce concentration when Keel spoke.

'Are you a nurse by profession?' he enquired.

Ros started violently. The question came out of the blue, and she was not prepared for it.

'No, I . . .' The bandage rolled from her hand, and she grabbed to retrieve it. Keel did the same with his good hand, and their fingers met and clenched round the errant white roll.

His touch stung like an electric probe, and Ros tried to jerk her hand away, but Keel's fingers were closed round her own and the bandage, and held them both tight.

She raised her eyes to his in angry protest, and colour flooded up her throat and cheeks in a rosy wave at the amusement she met in the tawny orbs, laughing at her confusion as he repeated his question,

'Are you a nurse?'

'No. I used to help my father. I still do, when I'm at home. He's a vet.'

Her disjointed answer released the bandage into her hand, and Ros lowered her eyes again quickly, and began to stroke the white cotton strip up and round and down, in the familiar figure of eight movement.

She concentrated on keeping the edges a neat half-inch apart, and slowly the familiar task began to calm her jangled nerves, and the colour started to recede from her hot cheeks, and she was able to control her reaction when Keel spoke again, though not her surprise at what he said.

'Your home life must have been very like my own.' He noted her quickly raised brows, and explained,

'My father's a surgeon.'

'Harley Street, I presume?' Ros parodied drily, and felt even more surprised when Keel shook his head, and said casually,

'No. Wenbury. It's a small market town lying under the lip of the Downs. It's a good life, there,' he added reflectively. 'Peaceful, and friendly.'

Ros's hands stilled at their task, and she stared up at him in open astonishment.

'Then why . . .' Words failed her, and she gestured round the well-appointed galley of the luxurious yacht. By most people's standards, the life Keel was leading away from Wenbury was more than good.

His lips lifted at her expression.

'I'd got no leaning towards the medical profession. My older brother followed my father, and my sister's a GP, but I wanted to see the world.'

He had more than achieved his ambition, Ros conceded. With a string of hotels to his name, plus a private jet and a yacht, the world had rewarded him handsomely. Fired by sudden curiosity, she could not resist asking, 'And now you've seen the world?'

'I like it. I like the challenge, and the excitement of battling against the odds, and coming out on top. But for a permanent base—a home—Wenbury wins every time.'

Was there, momentarily, a touch of wistfulness to the word 'home'? It must be the pain speaking. It was definitely not the Keel Ros knew. With an unexpected pang, she realised that she did not really know Keel at all. The man behind the tough, dynamic exterior was a closed book to her. It had taken a fire, and a badly burned arm, to reverse their relationship, and put her in even temporary charge of the situation, and surprise from Keel those unexpected details about himself and his background.

Unable to stop herself, Ros angled for more, with a statement that was in itself another question.

'You've got dozens of homes, all over the world. One in each of the hotels you own.'

'A hotel room isn't a home. It's an impersonal stopover. My home's at Wenbury. I've got a flat near my parents' house. I stay there as often as I can when I get back from my trips abroad.'

'You must feel like a chameleon, having to adjust constantly between two worlds.'

Ros sealed the end of the bandage with tape, and rose briskly to her feet, turning her back on Keel as she began to stack the unused equipment into the first-aid box.

'It's the same world. They're different people, that's all.'

She wondered which of the two lots of people he preferred.

His chair creaked as he rose, and she stiffened as she felt him come up behind her. She was hemmed in between him and the first-aid cupboard, and there was no room for her to turn away and get round him in the narrow galley.

She raised a hand to put a sterile dressing back in place in the cupboard, and it was more by luck than judgement that the unopened package landed on the shelf when Keel's voice murmured in her ear, 'Thank you, Ros.'

His arms closed round her, one on either side, bandage and all. The white, even folds of it were stark against her smoke-blackened cotton slacks as he drew her back to lean against him with a firmness that no badly burned arm had any right to show.

'F-for the dressing? That's all right,' she answered jerkily.

'And for helping me to beat out the fire.'

His lips nuzzled her neck, pushing aside her still damp hair, and Ros felt her spine bend, arching her against him.

'It wasn't a very big fire.'

It was a mere spark compared to the inferno his lips were setting alight inside her, and Ros drew in her breath with a painful catch.

'It might have burned you. Spoiled your beauty.'

'It didn't even scorch me.'

Instead, she was rapidly drowning in wave after wave of sensation as his lips travelled across the damp tendrils of her hair, across her shoulders to the silky skin of her arm.

'Keel . . .' Convulsively, Ros turned to face him.

'Do you want any help, Keel?' Footsteps clattered down the companionway, and a heavily French-accented voice demanded again, 'Do you want any help?' Keel's arms dropped from round her.

Hurriedly Ros hid her heightened colour in the first-aid cabinet, and was busily arranging the dressings and unused bandages in unnecessarily strict rotation when Jean-Jacques appeared in the galley.

'I've engaged automatic pilot for a minute or two

while I came down to check on you,' he explained.

'We've just finished,' Keel said casually. 'We were coming up to the wheelhouse to join you.'

Finished what? Ros wondered raggedly. Jean-Jacques's arrival had snapped the tenuous link between herself and Keel, briefly forged by the exchanged confidences. She ruminated on his disclosures as she stood beside him in the wheelhouse a few minutes later and sipped cautiously at the tot of rum which the Frenchman had insisted upon her drinking.

She grimaced at the taste, but she was grateful for the steadying effect of the spirits on her jangled nerves, and the way it eased the sickness she felt each time she thought about Keel's arm. She felt a craven gratitude that she would not have to dress it for a second time, for tomorrow the local doctor would have the unenviable task.

The white bandage on Keel's arm caused Milly to exclaim with horror when they appeared, dirty and bedraggled, on the terrace of the Casa some time later.

'I'll drive you to the hospital in town to have it dressed in the morning,' Walsh offered, but Keel refused.

'There's no need. Ros will do it for me.'

She spun sharply to confront him. 'I'm not a medic.' How many other jobs did he expect her to do around the Casa?

'You've got enough experience to dress a simple burn. There's no need to bother the hospital unless I think it's necessary.'

The bother would be hers. Ros cringed from the thought of removing the dressing in the morning. For once, she and Una were in complete agreement when the dark-haired girl said testily, 'If the burn's bad enough to need a dressing, it needs attention by a professional, not an amateur first-aider.'

'Keel will decide for himself, dear,' Milly put in, and Ros added a bitter, silent rider, as usual, as the artist went on, 'It's a long, hot drive into town and back. It'll be much better for Keel to have his arm dressed here, if Ros doesn't mind.'

Faced with Keel's determination, and Milly's obvious confidence in her ability, there was little Ros could do to extricate herself from the situation, but she minded very much.

The prospect of renewing the dressing gave her nightmares, the like of which she never suffered when helping her father to tend his furred and feathered patients, and the weary bruises under her eyes, that Milly said made her look ethereal, were accentuated as she nerved herself to face the unwelcome task the next morning.

The weather had changed overnight, bringing a blustery wind to drive the placid sea of yesterday into huge, white-capped combers on the beach below the house, and Keel's mood seemed to have changed to match.

He was back once more to being the dominant tycoon Ros was familiar with, and the confidences of yesterday might never have been as she bent her head over his arm, only to have him growl angrily, 'I thought you said the fire hadn't touched you? Your hair's scorched all down the one side. I told you to stay on board the *Sea Spray* where you'd be safe.'

'My hair was soaking wet from the sea. I didn't think it could scorch.'

'That falling branch would have set asbestos alight. You should have had more sense. It could spoil Milly's portrait.'

So it was Milly's portrait, and not her hair, that bothered him. Goaded to anger, Ros snapped, 'I wasn't to know the branch would fall.'

'It wouldn't have happened if you'd done as you were told.'

The fire would not have happened if Una had heeded Keel's warning about the tinder-dry state of the island, but Ros could not prove that it was the cigarette end that had set it alight, and, in any case, it was useless to say anything about it to Keel in his present mood.

'The portrait won't be affected,' she told him shortly. 'Milly's painting me from the other side.'

Resentment at his attitude helped her to ignore the faint pallor under Keel's healthy tan when she finished the painful dressing, a pallor that she knew must be reflected in her own cheeks as she tidied away the first-aid kit and went upstairs to change into the long violet dress in order to sit for Milly.

Her limpness was not assumed as she leaned back against the balustrade in the same pose she had affected yesterday, but the sitting proved to be short. The early morning wind was cool on the terrace, and because she had draped the cashmere shawl down the steps at her feet the day before, she could not put it across her shoulders now. Milly soon brought the session to an end with a rueful, 'I'm cold, and you must be, too. My fingers are too stiff to paint.'

Keel came on to the terrace as she spoke. Seeing them together, he turned away again, but Milly called him back.

'We've finished for this morning. The wind out here is too much, even for me.'

Keel turned back to join them. 'It's a good job it wasn't blowing yesterday, or we'd never have been able to put out the fire on the island. With a wind driving the flames, all that would have been left now would be a charred heap in the sea.'

'And that would have broken my heart.' Milly linked her arms companionably with Keel on her one side, and Ros on the other. 'It's my favourite view across the bay to the island, and I'd like to give each of you something special for saving it. No, I insist,' as their voices rose in joint protest. 'I thought, perhaps, a painting each? Choose any one you like.'

She looked enquiringly from one face to the other.

The painting of the windmill and the wild flowers flashed through Ros's mind. She had loved it at the exhibition, but she had also seen the price ticket attached to it and, however generous Milly's offer, she could not avail herself of such a costly gift. She was not Una.

Seeing her hesitate, Milly said kindly, 'Don't decide now. Think about it, and let me know. Now let's go in. Walsh has got plans for today.'

'I want to visit the caves on the other side of the island before I go back home,' the Canadian announced. 'If anyone hasn't seen them, they're welcome to come along.'

'That old tourist haunt,' Una snorted scornfully. 'There'll be absolutely crowds of people there.'

'That old tourist haunt happens to be one of the natural wonders of the world, and this tourist doesn't intend to miss it.' Walsh turned to Ros. 'Have you seen the caves?'

'No. I'd love to come with you.'

If she went alone with Milly and Walsh, it would take her out of Una's orbit, and away from Keel as well, she guessed. Walsh's next invitation justified her presumption that he would be otherwise occupied.

'What about you, Jean-Jacques?'

'I've seen the caves. They're wonderful,' the Frenchman enthused. 'I wouldn't mind seeing them again, but we'd planned to use the day giving the *Sea Spray* a trial run.'

'Anyone else?'

There were no other takers. Una's guests, it appeared, were going into town, and Una herself declared, 'I'm going on the *Sea Spray*.'

Her flashing eyes dared Keel to refuse her. Not that he would be likely to do so, Ros thought, and her lips curled as he smiled and said mildly, 'That's fine by me. We all seem to have sorted ourselves out nicely for the day.'

And astonished Ros beyond measure when, a short time later, with the yacht already well out to sea, he returned from the jetty and slid behind the wheel of the car that was to take them to the caves.

Ros stared at him with ill-concealed consternation. 'I thought Jean-Jacques said . . .'

'Jean-Jacques said we'd planned to use the day giving the *Sea Spray* a trial run. So we had. He's taking her right round the coast. He'll have a choppy run if this wind keeps up, but he's under instructions to keep her going until he's done at least one complete circuit, unless a mechanical fault crops up.'

Una had been under the impression that Keel would spend the day on the yacht as well. How furious she would be, when she discovered her mistake. By now, the *Sea Spray* would be well out of sight of land and, obeying Keel's orders, its skipper would refuse to put ashore until he was satisfied with the vessel's performance, which would take all day.

A bubble of laughter broke inside Ros and she gurgled irrepressibly, 'Can Una cook?'

'There'll be no need for her to prepare meals. Maria packed a hamper of food. But she'll have to brew the tea and wash up, because Jean-Jacques will be fully occupied at the wheel.'

Keel's face was studiedly blank, but his eyes were lit by twin devils of amusement, and Ros's laughter surfaced in an engaging chuckle that made the devils dance in response.

The small, shared joke seemed to break down the barrier between them and Ros relaxed back into her seat, prepared to enjoy the day.

Keel drove at a leisurely pace that gave his passengers plenty of time to gaze round them at the scenery. It was worthy of their attention. Their route took them along secondary roads, away from the tourist routes, and through tiny, unspoilt villages into the very heart of the island.

Colourful orange and lemon groves, heavy with fruit, passed by the car windows, to be succeeded by orchards of almond trees underplanted with cereal crops already in full ear, and scattered with a blaze of poppies turning vivid faces to follow the sun.

Sweet almonds, or bitter? Suddenly, Ros did not care.

Wild flowers made every untilled corner a patchwork of colour, and a windmill rose from the vivid carpet, an almost photographic replica of Milly's lovely painting.

'That's the windmill in my painting.' The artist pointed to it from the back of the car, and made Ros long more than ever to possess the canvas as a souvenir.

The only lack to her English ears was the sound of wild bird song. She commented upon it curiously, and Keel explained the, to her, unnatural silence.

'There are very few native wild birds on the island, except for gulls and sparrows, and an occasional hawk. There aren't any song birds, as we know them at home. They're mostly ground birds, such as quail and so on.'

It was a curious lack on this otherwise earthly paradise, and explained to Ros the caged birds that she had noticed twittering at almost every doorway in the villages and towns through which they passed.

She mourned their captivity, and Keel was quick to divert her attention.

'We've captured a nightingale,' he teased. 'Sing for

us.'

It was as natural for Ros to sing as it was for the birds and, moderating the volume of her voice to the close confines of the car, she let it flow softly where it willed as they drove along.

The rest of the journey fled, and it seemed no time at all before they joined the queue of sightseers trailing through the cave entrance in the wake of the guide.

The well-trodden pathway descended steeply into the bowels of the earth, and Ros strained her eyes, fearful of slipping in the dim light.

A high vaulted cavern rose above them, awesome in its petrified beauty, the delicate rock formations shown to their best advantage by inspired lighting. Ros gazed entranced, forgetting to watch where she trod, and was instantly punished for her carelessness when she slipped on a piece of wet rock.

The stumble splashed her legs, and Keel commanded her, 'Stand still while I dry you off.'

He shook out a spotless linen handkerchief and, ignoring Ros's shocked protest at its spoilage, proceeded to wipe off the muddy water. When it was done he pocketed the grubby square and said gravely, 'Now we're even. You dressed my arm, and I dried your leg.'

But his arm would require dressing again tomorrow. Ros shut her mind to the dreaded inevitability, and grasped at the coming diversion to distract her, as the path opened out in front of them to form an amphitheatre.

Rows of wooden benches looked down on to a wide underground lake, overhung by an incredible array of stalactites. The crowd splintered, intent on gaining their chosen seats, and Keel steered Ros on to a bench behind a row of schoolchildren, so that she had an unobstructed view over their heads at the water.

She turned enquiring eyes on his face. 'What happens now?'

'Wait and see.'

Ros shrugged. If he did not want to tell her, so be it. She began to leaf through her guidebook to find out for herself, when without warning all the lights went out.

The entombed darkness was total. It shocked the crowd into silence, and drew an involuntary gasp from Ros's lips. Instantly strong fingers wound round her own, folding her hand reassuringly in a warm, firm clasp.

The surrounding darkness, and the silence, were absolute. Bereft of the use of her eyes, Ros's other senses came sharply into play. She became aware of small rustles and shuffles from the people seated round her; aware of the sound of her own shallow breathing, and acutely conscious of Keel's deep, even breath, and the regular rise and fall of his ribcage against her arm, pushed into close contact by the seated crowd.

The voice of the guide broke through the darkness, explaining the musical pageant that was about to unfold before them from the lake, and lights began to glow from the rock formations bordering the water, softly at first, and then more brightly, gradual as the rising dawn.

They chased away the blackness to the nether regions of the cave, but still Keel's hand folded her own. Some deep instinct warned Ros that now or never was the time to pull away but, when she tried, his fingers tightened round her, refusing to release her.

She stole a swift glance at his face, but his eyes were intent on the small flotilla of boats that were gliding across the water in front of them, outlined with lights that made bright jewels of the myriad droplets flung up by their dipping oars.

The rowers sat in shadow, as did the musicians seated in the boats behind them, and music rose sweetly from the water, penetrating every corner of the vast cavern with sound. The boats carried the musicians to and fro, their music seeming to form a magic spell which bound their audience, and Ros's hand turned instinctively in Keel's grasp, and held his fingers in a tight grip.

His eyes turned swiftly to latch on to her face, but she was mesmerised by the pageant of the lake, and did not see. She felt unaccountably glad that she and Keel were sharing this moment of beauty together, but could not explained why, if anybody had asked.

The music faded, and died away, and Ros exhaled a long sigh as the boats began to disappear slowly, one after the other, back beyond the rock-lace curtain whence they had come.

Still held in thrall, she turned and looked up at Keel. His eyes locked with hers for a long immeasurable moment, and some unrecognisable thing inside her, which had its being in the sunny day and the witchery of the music, told her unmistakably which painting she must ask from Milly.

And it was not the painting of the windmill and the wild flowers.

CHAPTER SEVEN

DRESSING Keel's arm grew no easier by repetition. It was Ros who flinched, not her patient, and seeing it Keel scoffed.

'You're too soft-hearted.'

'Now you know why I'm not a nurse.'

His derision added to Ros's resentment that he should see her aversion, and still insist that she must continue the punishing task.

'Surely you don't object to doing this small amount of nursing—for me?'

Was the inflection deliberate, or was it simply her imagination? Ros had no time to ponder. As she taped the clean bandage to his wrist, Keel turned his hand over and grasped her fingers, and drew her towards him.

'I loathe it.'

Angrily she tried to jerk away, but although his arm was injured it had lost none of its strength, and he held her easily.

'Tell me why?' he invited, and his eyes and his voice were suddenly hard. 'You didn't mind dressing the servant's burn, so why should you mind dressing mine?'

How could she tell him, when she did not know the answer herself? Ros had dressed the manservant's arm with ease and despatch. Keel had waited and watched while she did it, and it was irrational to shrink from repeating the task on another arm.

But she had to find an answer to satisfy him in order to make him release her. The feel of his hand on her arm was doing peculiar things to her pulse rate, and in desperation she blurted out the first thing that came to her mind.

'It—it bores me,' she cried.

'Do *I* bore you?'

His voice was silky soft, so quiet that it took a second or two for Ros to register what he said, and another second for her to realise that Keel was handing her the perfect weapon with which to cut herself free.

She grasped it, and struck out.

'No——Yes.' She spoke recklessly, uncaring what she said so long as she made him loose her. 'Everything about this place bores me. The idleness. The pointlessness.'

Now the dam had burst, Ros was unable to stop, and the words poured over her trembling lips. 'Milly's the only one who seems to have any aim in life, or want one.'

It was as untrue as it was unjust, and she knew it.

Her accusation applied to Una and her set, but not to Keel or Walsh. But the words were out, and she could not draw them back, and they had the desired effect. Slowly Keel's arms dropped to his sides, releasing her. His face was set, and pale under its tan, but that could have been the after-effects of the painful dressing.

Through tight lips he gritted, 'I won't bore you again,' and pivoting on his heel he turned and left the room, pulling the door to behind him with a final-sounding slam.

Ros did not discover who renewed his dressings after that. He disappeared each morning for a couple of hours, and returned with a fresh bandage on his arm. Soon, however, the natural healing powers of his own superb physical condition asserted themselves, and he was able to dispense with the bandages, as he had with Ros's help.

Perversely, she discovered that she missed the daily sessions alone with Keel, but after their quarrel she did not see him on his own again.

The sense of strain between them grew, ably abetted by Una, who openly flaunted her ability to claim his attention. As the days went by, Ros and Keel ceased speaking to one another unless driven to do so by the politeness of convention.

During the day, Jean-Jacques claimed Keel's attention to work on the yacht, and in the evenings Una monopolised him. When he and Ros did accidentally find themselves together for a moment or two, he was icily polite, and removed himself from her side at the earliest opportunity.

The days dragged. Posing for Milly helped Ros to get through the mornings, but this, too, soon came to an end. After one particularly long session, Milly exclaimed with a stretch of relief, 'That's it. I shan't need you to pose for me again. I've done all I can to the portrait. There are only bits of the background still to be touched up, and I shan't need you for those.'

While Milly was preoccupied with finishing her painting, Maria turned to Ros for support in the day-to-day running of the Casa, but when the portrait was finished and Milly was free to take charge again, Ros knew her time there had come to an end.

Quietly, she made her plans.

Her return flight ticket was open-ended, and she was fortunate in finding a cancellation on a direct flight to London the next morning. She said nothing to Milly about her intentions. She would broach her plans to the artist during the evening when there would be no time for Milly to cajole her into staying on.

It was a depleted party that took dinner on the terrace and the rest were to follow on the morrow, with Walsh going as well soon afterwards. There was no mention of Una leaving.

If their numbers were smaller than usual, the guests made up for it by their gaiety. They persuaded a village band, on its way home from a wedding, to remain and play for the dancing, and the bright, gypsy-style costumes lent an air of festival to the last evening together.

The secret of her booked flight home the next day weighed upon Ros's mind during dinner, but amid the general chatter was no time to confide it to Milly, and she joined in the general discussion about the forthcoming art exhibition in New York as if she had not a care in the world.

In spite of her guests' pleading, Milly was adamant in her refusal to show them her canvas, only promising, 'I'll send you all complimentary tickets to the exhibition. Come and see the portrait there, for yourselves.'

No one seemed to notice Ros's lack of response, and after the meal ended, the band struck up, and she danced, and tried to look as if she enjoyed it.

Some inexplicable impulse had made her don the long violet dress for this one last evening, an impulse she did not try to explain even to herself, and which she regretted immediately when Keel came up to her and said abruptly, 'You'll never have another dress that suits you better.'

He was so sure of himself. So arrogantly sure that he was always in the right, even to the point of choosing other people's clothes. Ros tilted her chin at him defiantly.

'I've got lots of dresses I like better.'

For most of the evening she had managed to successfully avoid dancing with Keel. Una's guests made eager partners, and the hour was growing late when he eventually captured her for a quickstep, and growled ill-humouredly, 'Does it amuse you to play hard to get?'

Ros raised a clear violet stare, innocent of guile. 'I don't know what you mean. I'm here to help Milly to act as hostess.' Her voice held an unconsciously bitter note as she added, 'That's what I'm being paid for.'

'You're not paid to devote all your time to the crowd Una's gathered round her.'

'A hostess has to dance with all the guests.'

'I'm a guest. I'm entitled to an equal share of your attention.'

'This quickstep's your share.' The quicker it was over, the better, she added silently.

'I'll have the last waltz as well.'

The music changed, but Keel retained a firm hold on her wrist and pulled her back masterfully into his arms with a sharp, 'At least try to pretend you're enjoying yourself, if only to please Milly.'

Ros's voice cut as she retorted, 'I'm enjoying the *music*.'

To prove it she began to hum the waltz tune under her breath, and was startled when a baritone rumble through Keel's chest joined in. The notes soared together, and Ros's eyes flew up to his face.

Tawny orbs gazed deep down into violet, piercing, probing. Defensively Ros forced a smile to her lips, and made them form the words of the song,

'I'll dance the last waltz with you.'

It was the last waltz she would ever be obliged to dance with Keel, and she would show him that she was glad . . . glad . . .

The gladness did not bring the expected sense of elation as the dance ended and Keel released her, and Milly called upon her to sing while the band refreshed themselves. Instead, pain invaded her voice as she sang,

'Falling in love is wonderful . . .'

Who was the songwriter kidding? she thought cynically, and changed the song for another, which was just as pointless because she no longer believed in love.

'When I fall in love, it will be for ever. When I fall in love with you.'

Her love had not lasted for long, let alone for ever, and the agony of disillusion loaded her voice as she sang, vibrating through the words with a raw pain she was unable to conceal, until the very intensity of her singing stilled the chatter on the terrace, and every word dropped like a stone into a pool of listening silence.

Her voice broke finally on the last, throbbing notes, as the band returned to play again. Keel pushed himself upright from where he had leaned to listen on the terrace balustrade. His face was harsh and set, and his voice was a cold snarl of anger as he turned on Ros.

'You must be missing some man pretty badly, to sing like that.'

How little he knew. Where Lomas had been was now only a bleak emptiness, and there was no one to fill it, but in self-defence Ros lied bravely.

'I do. I'm leaving here tomorrow. Going back home.' Inferring without words that there would be someone special waiting for her when she returned.

'If you feel so badly, why didn't you go before?' Keel turned abruptly to Una. 'Let's dance.' He circled the dark-haired girl away in his arms and left Ros standing on the terrace on her own, feeling suddenly, achingly lonely.

Milly protested at the news that she intended to leave, as Ros had guessed she would, but she was adamant in her determination to go and, making packing her excuse, she escaped to her room.

Slowly she took off the long violet dress. Although she intended to pay for it, she felt she never wanted to see it again. She hung it in the wardrobe and shut the door on it. The maid would find it there when she came to clean the room. She was welcome to keep it.

Ros burned with humiliation as she remembered her conversation with Milly, when the artist had taken her aside on learning that she intended to leave the following morning. She had tried her hardest to persuade Ros to remain, and then, when she saw that her efforts were getting her nowhere, had said plaintively, 'I don't want you to go, my dear. I shall miss you so much. But if you feel you really must, I'll let you have the payment we agreed.'

'You must deduct the money that's debited to your account for the clothes I brought when I went to town that day.'

'I wouldn't dream of it.'

'I insist.' On this point, too, Ros had refused to be moved, and again Milly had had to capitulate reluctantly.

'Oh, well, if you really want me to. But the modest cost of a few cotton garments . . .'

'This evening dress isn't made of cotton, and the cost of it was far from modest.'

'The dress isn't down to my account. Didn't you know? Keel bought that for you; he was so taken by the way the colour matches your eyes.'

In that case, Ros fumed, Keel could have it back.

She felt so angry, it was all she could do not to tear the hated dress from off her back there and then, and hurl it across the terrace at him. The violence of her feelings stormed her through her packing in record time, and with nothing else left to do she wandered restlessly on to the balcony of her room.

The party on the terrace was breaking up. Una's guests were following Ros's example and repairing to their rooms. She leaned against the window frame, keeping out of sight, and saw Una and Keel stroll off together through the pine wood, as if they might be making for the beach.

A few minutes later, Milly and Walsh followed them, and Ros thought humourlessly, 'They won't be popular if they catch up.' Which would not be long, she judged, if Milly continued to walk with such a brisk step, much faster than her usual sedate pace. Perhaps the artist felt more energetic than usual in the cooler night air.

Silence descended on the Casa after they had gone, but still Ros did not stir from her leaning post. She felt drained. Even her anger had subsided, leaving a curious emptiness inside her.

After a long interval the band reappeared, coming from the kitchen quarters, where they had evidently been given a late supper by Maria before starting out on their journey home to their own village.

Undaunted by the distance they had still to go, the violinist raised his bow, and the gaily costumed little band strolled away, singing lustily as they went.

'Play, gypsy. Teach me to smile . . .'

The words floated back to her through the darkened pine woods, haunting, hurting, bringing back stray memories of the last weeks on Majorca.

'Buy a flower for the lady, for luck.'

'Haven't you ever been kissed before?'

'Buy a flower for the lady . . .'

The red carnation had not lived up to its promise,
Ros thought bitterly. Even so she could not bring
herself to throw it away, and tucked it in the secret
depths of her suitcase, pressed between the pages of
a book.

'Play, gypsy . . .'

The fitful wind gusted the high, sweet notes of the
fiddle back to Ros like tiny darts, reminding her that
she had little to smile about, with no job to return to
in England, and little prospect of one, and with the
money she had earned in Majorca squandered on
clothes she did not need, and did not want.

'Play, gypsy. Teach me to smile.'

Ros raised her hands to her face, as if to ward off
the persistent, stabbing missiles, but still they came,
and the wind laughed heartlessly when, for no
reason she could think of, the tears came, and
streamed down her cheeks like rain.

The next morning she used make-up to disguise the
ravages of the storm the night before. She had one
final task to do before she left the Casa, and she set
about it tight-lipped.

Among the telephone calls she had made the day
before had been one to the store in town to discover
the exact cost of the long violet evening dress. She
knew it would be high, but even so the figure when
she received it made her gasp. It still gave her a sense
of unbelief as she wrote it down carefully on a piece
of Milly's pink writing paper, adding the shawl and
the carnation underneath.

Together, the total added up to almost all of the rest
of the money she had received from Milly the night

before. The lunch Keel had given her she ignored; he had not had to pay for it in his own hotel.

The impromptu statement finished, she carefully folded the appropriate currency notes to cover the total, and sealed them together in an envelope and addressed it to Keel. She did not use a cheque in case he might refuse to cash it, and deny her the satisfaction of her gesture of independence.

Now she was ready to leave. Her case had already been taken from her room, and she went downstairs to join the other guests who were likewise going to the airport in the minibus.

Milly kissed her warmly. 'I'll see you at the exhibition. I'll have your own painting ready for you by then.'

She would never receive the painting. Ros had long since regretted the impulse that had prompted her to ask for it but, since she would not be going to the exhibition, she would not be faced with the embarrassment of being obliged to accept it.

She had not the heart to disillusion Milly, and turned with relief to Walsh as the Canadian held out his hand.

'I thought you were driving us to the airport?' she said, shaking it warmly.

'Keel's driving you instead. Milly and I are going to spend a last day out together before I have to go home as well.'

There was no mention of Una. Perhaps she was coming with them in the minibus? Ros had not seen the black-haired girl that morning, and she fingered the envelope in her pocket with a sinking heart.

Una's presence would make it doubly difficult for her to give it to Keel. When he knew what it contained, he would be furiously angry, and her courage wavered at the prospect of handing it to him.

She did not relish the battle that was bound to ensue, but it was one she had to win for the sake of her own self-respect. She climbed into the minibus and took a seat right at the back. Keel shot her a keen look as he slid behind the wheel, but he did not speak. He set the bus rolling, still with Una not on board.

Ros waved with the others to Milly and Walsh, and wished nervously she had left the envelope of money with the latter to give to Keel when he got back, but it was too late now. Her tension grew as they neared the airport, and she planned her strategy carefully.

Without Una there, Keel would be unlikely to linger with the other girl's guests. He had no cause to want to linger with herself. She would stay with the rest of the departing group until the very last minute, and slide the envelope into Keel's hand just as he was about to leave, then escape into the departure lounge, where he would not be able to follow her.

It might have worked if she had not been in the back seat of the minibus. By the time she had followed the others out, Keel had her suitcase firmly in his grip and, with a casual, 'Goodbye. Have a safe journey,' to the others, he took her by the arm and steered her determindly to the check-in point.

'I can manage on my own,' Ros protested, but he held on to her case, and perforce she had to remain with him to see it safely through. It disappeared on the moving conveyor belt, and Keel said,

'You've got time for a coffee.'

'I don't want one now. I'll have one on the plane.'

A coffee, *tête-à-tête* with him, was the last thing she wanted. The envelope containing the money burned a hole in her pocket, and she longed to be rid of it and away before he had time to open it. A volcanic eruption would be as nothing compared to what would happen when he discovered its contents, and she wanted to be out of the firing-line when the explosion occurred.

'I'll go. I want to get some duty-frees,' she said hurriedly.

She had not got enough money left to indulge in duty-frees, but it was as good an excuse as any, and not one he could argue with. Ros's fingers closed convulsively over the envelope. Now was the time to give it to him. Now, in the entrance to the departure lounge, with the baggage X-ray check only inches away, and offering the perfect escape route.

She felt like a prisoner about to scale the gaol wall as she measured the distance with her eyes, and her heart hammered painfully against her ribs as she raised them to his face and saw that Keel was doing the same, almost as if he suspected what was going through her mind, Ros thought with rising panic.

When he began in a harsh sounding voice, 'Ros, I . . .' her nerve broke. Taking a deep breath, she pulled the envelope out of her pocket and pressed it into his hand.

'I must go. Goodbye,' she gabbled and, pushing

her hand-luggage through the X-ray machine, she almost ran through the barrier.

Several yards inside safety, she turned and looked back. Keel still stood where she had left him, as still as if he was carved in stone. His face was chalk white underneath his tan, and his fingers balled the envelope in his fist, as if intent on crushing the very life out of it. That he knew its contents was evident from the ear of pink paper that peeped through one of his fingers.

Ros shivered, and felt suddenly sick with reaction.

Instinctively she shrank back as Keel's hand came up, as if in the heat of his fury he might hurl the envelope and the money it contained after her, but just then a group of laughing holidaymakers crowded into the departure entrance, and momentarily he was engulfed. When they disappeared he was gone and Ros collapsed on to the first available seat in the departure lounge from legs that suddenly refused to support her.

A small pile of post awaited her on her return to the flat.

One letter, dated a week ago, was from Sally, to say that her friend had been offered a job with accommodation in the north of England, and would not be returning to the flat. Silently, Ros wished her luck and started to read another. It was from her mother, and said, 'Your father's got a new assistant. I've had to put him in your room for the moment while the boys are at home on vacation.'

Which meant that she either had to find another

flatmate or face leaving, since she could not possibly afford to remain there on her own. And for the moment at any rate, she was denied even a brief visit home, since her room would be occupied.

Black depression gripped Ros. The weather had remained cold, and she shivered after the warmth of Majorca, but dared not be too liberal with the heating because of the cost.

She was reluctant to replace Sally's cheerful companionship with that of a stranger, and it would be difficult, if not impossible, to find cheaper accommodation of a similar standard, so to tide her over she took whatever temporary work was on offer, in order to pay the whole of the rent herself until she decided what to do.

Spring dragged into summer with one short-lived job after another, and Ros was almost at the end of her tether one morning when two more envelopes dropped through her letter box.

The one was a warning from her landlord of a huge, and imminent rent rise. The other was from Milly; it contained a complimentary ticket to the art exhibition, an air ticket, and a booking in Ros's name at the hotel in New York. A scribbled note on the back of the ticket said, 'No need to write. Just arrive. We've all missed you.'

By all, the artist must mean herself. No one else, least of all Keel and Una, would miss her. Ros's hand was already reaching for notepaper and pen to send her excuses, when she paused.

Why should she not go to the exhibition?

There was nothing to keep her in England. She had

no permanent job, and no immediate prospect of one. Soon, she would have no roof over her head. The rent rise would have stretched her income, even with a flatmate and a regular job. In her present circumstances, it was right out of her reach.

So, why not go to New York? It would give her time to think, and plan ahead. She quaked at the prospect of meeting Keel again, but by now, after all these weeks, his anger must have cooled, and he was more likely to avoid her than to seek her company.

She might even find a job in America, as an *au pair*. The thought cheered her. It was worth a try.

Ros did not lack courage. Once she had made up her mind, she acted swiftly. She rang her family to tell them of her plans, cancelled her tenancy of the flat, and three days later she landed in New York.

A hire car was at the airport to meet her, but no one was with it except the driver, and she sighed her relief as she rode in solitary state to the hotel. She still had a few hours' respite before she was obliged to meet Keel again.

A scribbled note from Milly, 'We're all at the gallery. See you at dinner,' was a small warmth to welcome her, and Ros dressed for the meal as if she was donning armour.

She tried unsuccessfully to laugh off the clammy feel of her palms that reduced her crisp lace handkerchief to a crumpled rag when she could no longer put off descending the stairs, and her stomach curled into a tight knot as she stepped on to the first one.

Keel stood on the polished parquet floor below,

looking up, and watched her descend.

In spite of her determination to remain calm and aloof, Ros's hand sought the banister rail for support. She began to count the stairs in order to help her to resist the impact of his eyes, but her mind refused to retain the sequence of the numbers, and as her suddenly fumbling feet took her down the last step, they brought her up against Keel.

He did not move aside to allow her to pass, and perforce Ros had to stop. She flung back her head in haughty protest that he should so deliberately block her way; flashing violet eyes met burning amber, and she knew with unnerving certainty that, while she had been back in England, nothing had changed. Keel was still as furious with her now as when she had left him at the airport all those weeks ago.

CHAPTER EIGHT

WALSH rescued her. He strolled across from where he and Milly were sitting in the lobby, put a glass in Ros's hand, and said cheerily, 'You're just in time for a drink before dinner. I remember you liked this when you were at the Casa. It isn't too strong.'

It was not nearly strong enough to shield her from Keel's anger. When Walsh took her by the arm and chided Keel unnecessarily, 'Don't monopolise her. Milly's longing to see her again,' she could feel Keel's eyes lance down like twin swords on the top of her head as he stepped aside to allow her to walk past him.

Milly's obvious delight at their meeting made a small warm patch to counteract Keel's stony lack of greeting, and to Ros's relief dinner turned out to be a social affair, with many of the other artists who were exhibiting at the gallery joining them for the evening.

Ros found herself absorbed into a friendly group sitting umpteen places away from Keel. Una was not present, and the girl's absence puzzled her, but she shrugged it aside as an added blessing, and as soon as dinner was over, she excused herself on the grounds of jet-lag, and escaped to her room.

Once there, however, she discovered that, while she was out of Keel's sight, she was not out of his range. She walked over to her dressing-table to remove her watch preparatory to getting undressed, and saw on its top a neatly wrapped parcel addressed to herself.

Curious, she carried it over to her bed. Surely this could not be the painting Milly had promised her? It looked far too large. She pulled off the wrappings to reveal layers of tissue paper, and sudden premonition made her fingers start to tremble.

Underneath lay deep violet silk, and paler violet cashmere. On top of the dress and the shawl lay the shortest of notes, written in a strong, dominant hand that could only belong to Keel. It said curtly, 'Milly's supplying the pearls.'

It was not signed. It did not need to be. The strong penstrokes betrayed their author as surely as a finger-print, and black fury choked Ros as she glared down at them, as if the heat of her anger would burn the marks from off the paper.

No matter how she fought him, Keel still presumed to dictate to her what she should wear. She would tell him exactly what he could do with his orders, right now. Furiously she jumped to her feet, and the movement sent the evening dress and shawl spilling from her lap across the carpet, tangling with her feet, so that she was obliged to stop and pick them up to save herself from falling.

The small delay brought reason flooding back. Keel was presumably still with the rest of the party, and she could not create a scene in public. She flung the hated garments from her on to a chair, and promised herself grimly, I'll tackle him very first thing tomorrow morning.

If he was still angry with her for returning the money

to him, he would discover that her own anger far outmatched his.

The next morning Ros hurried downstairs early, with the rewrapped parcel in her hands, and the light of battle in her eyes. She ran into Keel in the lobby.

'You can have this back,' she told him without preamble, and thrust the parcel at him.

Taken by surprise, any other person would have reached out and taken it. But not Keel. He slid his hands deep into the pockets of his slim-fitting slacks, and regarded Ros coolly from his superior height.

'You'll need them to wear for the exhibition this evening.'

'I'll go in my own clothes. I don't need you to tell me what to wear.'

His eyes narrowed to tawny slits. 'Let's get one thing straight. I don't care what you dress in. It doesn't interest me. So far as I'm concerned you can come in your bikini. In fact . . .' A grin split his lips that more nearly resembled a snarl, since no humour softened the agate hardness of his eyes. 'In fact, it might liven up the proceedings a bit if you did.'

He ignored her outraged gasp and swept on, 'If you're to be of any use to Milly, you've got to reflect the portrait she painted of you so that the judges can see what a superb job she's made of it. You can't do that if you're dressed in different clothes. Why else did you think I bothered to bring them?'

His voice cut like a whiplash, and Ros almost put a hand up to her cheek, so sharp was the impression of a blow, as he went on grimly, 'If you don't intend to help Milly, why did you come? Unless it was simply for the pleasure of ruining her chances?'

'Of course not. I wouldn't stoop to such a thing.' Did he judge all women by Una's standards?

'Think about it,' he advised her curtly as Walsh strolled up to them and enquired, 'What is everyone doing today?'

'I've got a board meeting to attend,' Keel answered, and added with a steely look at Ros, 'Whatever you believe, we're not all idle.'

So it still rankled, that she had likened him to Una's playboy companions. The realisation gave Ros a perverse satisfaction, that at least he had taken that much notice of what she had said.

Milly came to join them and begged plaintively, 'Will somebody please take Walsh out for the day? I've got lots to do at the gallery, and I simply can't have him under my feet.'

'That leaves you and me, Ros,' the Canadian grinned. 'Let's get out of the way of these busy people, and go off somewhere together. That is, unless you've got any plans?'

Ros's one ambition at that moment was to get out of Keel's way. Her plans had embraced the local employment agencies, but in her present mood she did not feel at her most persuasive so far as interviews were concerned, and her eagerness was genuine when she said, 'No plans. I'd love to come.'

She could relax with Walsh. He was an undemanding companion, and anything was better than running the risk of bumping into Keel if he should happen to finish his meeting early.

Walsh called after her, 'Dress easy,' as she made her

way upstairs to get ready, then turned back to talk to Keel. Ros interpreted the advice into a sage-green trouser suit and a honey-coloured silk sweater, that the Canadian's appreciative look approved as she settled beside him in the American-sized car shortly afterwards.

'It's enormous,' Ros exclaimed, settling back. 'Why are all cars so big over here?'

'It's a big country. It makes the folks think big.'

Keel came from England, a small enough country compared to this, but he thought big, in terms of real pearls instead of artificial ones.

Walsh drove steadily out of the city's dense traffic, and in deference to his need to concentrate Ros remained silent. Soon they left the towering office blocks behind them and, glancing back, she wondered in which of them Keel was holding his meeting.

She could visualise him chairing the board, a strong man leading other strong men, sure of his facts and figures, of what he wanted to do, and where he wanted to go.

Hastily Ros switched her thoughts to another subject.

'Where are we heading for?' She felt free to speak now that the city was left behind and gentler scenery showed through the car windows as it ate up the miles.

'A place where we can get some fresh air and exercise,' the Canadian answered obscurely. 'You do ride, don't you?'

'As often as I can. Not recently, though.'

'We'll remedy that today,' Walsh promised, and shortly afterwards pulled the car off the road on to a dirt track that led them to a low, ranch-style building, with a board notice that proclaimed it to be a hotel. It was a place of some substance, Ros saw, and its state of upkeep spoke of caring and affluent owners.

Well tended gardens surrounded the building, with patios dotted with comfortable loungers, and the surrounding scenery invited riding parties. Low hills relieved lush grassland, and in the distance a river gleamed.

'It's a dude ranch,' Walsh enlightened her. 'It's very popular with folk who want to get out of the city for a few hours, but can't afford the time to go too far away. It was Keel's idea.'

'Keel's?' A numb feeling of inevitability began to take hold of Ros.

'Yes. He saw the need, and he bought up the old house and restored it, adding all mod cons. Business has gone like a bomb ever since. This is where he held the board meeting this morning.'

'Here?' Ros's voice cracked on her dismay.

'Yes. When we were talking after breakfast, he suggested bringing you out here for an afternoon on horseback.'

Keel was still at it, Ros realised in furious disbelief. Even on her day out with Walsh, he was dictating what she would do to occupy her time. Was he still here at the hotel? If so, she would give him a piece of her mind to let him know what she thought of his arrogant dictation.

Barely had the question formed in her mind, than Keel himself answered it.

He emerged from a pair of wide-flung glass doors and strolled to meet them, and to Ros's consternation he was dressed in riding kit. Her eyes riveted on the nut-brown breeches moulding into polished, handmade riding boots, and matching brown open-necked shirt, and her glance rose to do battle with his enigmatic stare.

He had planned it all, to the extent of having appropriate dress himself for the occasion, which told her that he intended to ride with them. In that case, he could count her out of the party, she thought furiously, and glared as he approached her, while Walsh trotted off happily to inspect the block of nearby stables.

'I don't need you to organise my entertainment for me,' she told him abruptly. 'I pay for that, like I pay for my own clothes.'

His face tightened, and he thrust one hand deep into his pocket. 'You already have paid for it,' he gritted. 'Every last cent. Or should I say, peseta? Likewise your air ticket, and your hotel bill. And here's your change.'

His hand came out of his pocket gripping a coin. Before Ros could back out of his reach, he reached out and grabbed her hand, and prised it open palm upwards, before slapping a five peseta coin into it with a stinging force that made her wince.

Ros hardly heard the clatter of hooves on the cobbled yard as Walsh and a groom brought out three horses towards them.

White-faced, she stared from Keel to the coin in her hand. She had paid for her own ride, and everything else. Or, more correctly, Keel had paid with the money she had given back to him. Every last peseta, except five.

The coin seemed to mock her, sitting in the middle of her palm that was still red from the force of Keel's slap.

He had spent the money on her, which meant that he himself had still paid for the evening dress and the shawl, which, unless she was to jeopardise Milly's chances at the exhibition tonight, she must weat to reflect her portrait.

They were back to square one.

Through a mist of anger she heard Walsh call cheerfully to Keel, 'Ros does ride. You said she would.'

'As a vet's daughter, I was sure she must.'

As usual, Keel's judgment was flawless, so accurate that it left no room for guesswork. She hated him for it, and herself for not being able to shout back truthfully, 'I don't ride. I don't know one end of a saddle from the other.' But because she could ride was no good reason why she should give in to Keel and ride now. Her chin tilted, and she fought back.

'I do ride, but I don't want to this afternoon. It—it's too warm.'

'Aw, honey, don't let me down,' Walsh expostulated. 'I've been looking forward to taking you to see my favourite view along the river here.'

Keel remained silent, but his eyes bored into her, and said as clearly as if he had spoken, 'Are you going to spoil things for Walsh as well?'

'Keel will lend you a stetson, to keep off the sun,' Walsh begged. 'You'll look great in a stetson.'

Ros felt trapped. It was as if there was some massive intrigue working against her, designed to make sure she must always submit to Keel's will, and she had to fight it, and win, if she was to survive.

His eyes monitored her silent battle, and then, after what seemed an age, he turned. 'I'll get you a hat,' he said, as if the result was a foregone conclusion, and Ros felt the bitter taste of defeat in her mouth when Walsh exulted,

'Atta girl. The sun won't give you freckles if you wear a hat.'

In fact, the sun was only pleasantly warm. Ros left her jacket in the car, and pushed up the sleeves of her sweater to bare her arms to the kindly rays as the groom walked the horses towards her.

The mounts were of the same quality as their surroundings, she saw, and she could not subdue a stirring of excitement as she watched them. Keel had not insulted her by offering her a plodder to ride.

The tall chestnut mare whose reins the groom offered to her had alert, pricked ears, and a high-stepping gait. Ros gazed at it and was lost. This was a far cry from the riding stable hacks she normally had to make do with, and her heart beat with excitement at the thought of topping such a mount.

Keel came back, and nodded dismissal to the groom. 'Thanks, Jack. I'll give Miss Morland a lift up.'

He dangled a white stetson hat from his fingers Ros saw. 'I don't need a lift,' she snapped.

Keel could keep his help. And his hat. If he was so sure she could ride a horse of the calibre he had provided for her, he must also realise that she was not such a novice as to need his help in mounting it, and independently she set out to prove it.

Swift as a thought she slotted her foot into the stirrup, reached up for the high pommel of the saddle, and tried to haul herself aboard.

It proved to be unexpectedly difficult.

The mare was tall. The stirrups were enclosed, and felt awkward and ungainly on her foot. The leathers were Western-style length, much longer than those she was accustomed to, so that she had to stretch up much further to get her leg up and over the high curved contours of the ranch saddle, a manoeuvre not helped by her closely tailored slacks, which restricted her movement in a way that jodhpurs would not have done.

To her chagrin, Ros discovered her leg was inches too short to achieve her objective and, panting and furious, she slid back helplessly to the ground as Keel strode up behind her.

He said abruptly, 'If you'd waited for me to help you . . .'

'I don't need your help. I don't want it,' she emphasised, in case he should misunderstand her, and saw by the sudden tightening of his jaw that he had understood her very clearly. 'All I need is to shorten the leathers a bit.'

'I'll do it for you.'

'I can do it myself.'

'I'd hate you to break your nails. You might need them to scratch with.'

For nails, read claws. Ros drew in her breath with a sharp hiss that was not unlike the sound of a furious cat, and Keel's eyes flicked to her face, but before she could speak he drawled, 'Put on your hat, while I see to the tackle.'

His own hand was as quick as a cat's paw, and Ros had no time to dodge as he dropped the stetson on to her head and gave it a couple of sharp taps on top.

It was deliberate. It had to be. The first tap pushed the hat over her eyes, blocking out her vision. The second wedged the headgear tightly over her ears.

Ros yelled at him furiously, 'Get me out of this thing. I can't see.'

She ground her teeth as Keel's refusal penetrated the felty darkness. 'Get yourself out of it. It'll keep you occupied while I go to work on the stirrup strap.'

She would go to work on him, Ros fumed, the second she could see again.

Grasping the wide brim with both hands, she gave the hat a mighty tug, and it slid off her shining gold waves so swiftly that she was unable to prevent the cord from coming up under the end of her nose, with a tweak that brought tears to her eyes.

'You . . . You . . .' She loathed Keel for the derision that lit his eyes, and longed to lash out with her foot as he bent to hoist her into the saddle, but with quick intuition he divined her intention, and swiftly jack-knifed her leg, preventing her from kicking back.

'I'm used to handling high-spirited mares,' he taunted and, ducking his head under the wide stetson brim, he kissed her hard on the mouth. The next second, he had launched her high into the saddle.

If she had carried a riding crop, she would have struck him. Failing a weapon, Ros lashed him with her eyes, but his own mocked her futility, and he turned away and vaulted lightly on to the back of a large grey stallion.

Walsh rode in front, guiding them to his favourite view, and Keel rode beside Ros. Horse and rider were both taller than she and her mare, towering above her so that she felt as if she was in custody as her mount stepped docilely beside the grey, so accustomed to the route that it needed no guidance from her.

The sun was gently warm, and the scenery was green and restful, but there was no rest in it for Ros. Her lips throbbed from Keel's bruising kiss, and frustration added fuel to her anger as she rode beside him.

The bright waters of the river danced and sang beside them as they cantered along its banks, but for once she could find no answering music inside herself, and when Walsh proudly pointed out his favourite view she intoned automatically, 'How lovely,' her anger blurring the green vista so that she scarcely knew if she was looking in the right direction or not.

'You're quiet, honey,' the Canadian noticed at length. 'Are you tired?'

'Perhaps. Just a little,' Ros excused her lack of response, and Walsh turned his horse and considerately led the way back towards the ranch.

'Or perhaps you're bored?'

Keel's voice lashed her, biting for all its low tone so that Walsh, riding in front of them, should not hear.

Ros flashed back, 'Perhaps I am,' and, touching the mare's flanks with her heels, she sent the lively creature at a fast canter to catch up with Walsh, leaving Keel behind.

That evening Ros dressed herself in the long violet dress. It would be the very last time she was obliged to wear it. She averted her eyes from the mirror as she clasped Milly's pearls round her throat and wrist, and turned to the artist for inspection.

'I'm so excited,' Milly bubbled. 'This is a really big

day for me. It's quite something just to have a portrait hung at this exhibition, whether or not it comes first.'

'I can't wait to see it.'

'All you have to do is to look in the mirror, my dear. You look just perfect.'

Ros did not want to look in the mirror. She felt she never wanted to set eyes on the hated dress and shawl again, and anger still burned in her like a destroying fire when she entered the art gallery some time later with Milly and Walsh.

Keel was there before them. She had not seen him since she had left him at the dude ranch to come back to the hotel with Walsh, and after one all-encompassing glance to make sure she was wearing what he intended, he turned back to resume talking to the group of people with him, and ignored her.

Pointedly, Ros turned away and toured the gallery in the opposite direction. All the portraits were hung along the walls, and the coveted place at the head of the gallery remained tantalisingly empty.

She wondered which painting would occupy it at the end of the evening, and could not restrain her curiosity to see what Milly had made of the portrait.

Although she had seen many examples of the artist's work, Ros was still unprepared when she came to a halt in front of the painting. It was outstanding. The likeness was as real as if she was, indeed, looking at herself in the mirror.

Without exaggeration, the portrait was a masterpiece.

But it was hung among other masterpieces from some of the world's most famous artists, and silently Ros wished it luck as she stepped aside to make way for the party of judges, who were making the last of their numerous tours of the room, trying to make what she thought must be an almost impossible choice among so much talent.

They came closer, and stopped in front of Milly's portrait, and impulsively Ros acted. What drove her to do it, she did not pause to consider. Perhaps it was one last gesture of defiance at Keel, to prove to him that her principles were not on the same level as those of Una. Perhaps it was, simply, her very real affection for Milly.

The artist's portrait was hung close beside a small stairway leading on to a raised platform that served as a stage. Just such a flight of steps, in fact, as Ros had sat atop on the terrace at the Casa, to pose for Milly.

The judges talked together in low tones, and Ros's sense of the dramatic took hold of her. In a gesture that would have brought applause from her fellow members of the amateur operatic society, and yet seemed to Ros to be as natural as breathing, she sank on to the top step, leaned back against the small post supporting the handrail, and trailed her cashmere shawl down the remaining steps at her feet, in an exact duplicate of the pose she used for Milly.

One of the judges exclaimed, 'This has got to be the one,' and his eyes went from the portrait to Ros, and back again. 'The likeness is so perfect, I scarcely know which is the portrait, and which is the model.'

Applause exploded round her. Milly unashamedly hugged her, and Press and television crowded round, demanding Ros should sit under the portrait and be photographed over and over again.

With much ceremony, the portrait was then taken

from its place on the wall, and hung in the place of honour at the head of the gallery, and Milly's lifelong ambition was achieved.

Keel came over and embraced the artist, and then he turned to Ros.

'Congratulations,' he said.

'For what?' she retorted coolly. 'The portrait's a masterpiece. It won on its merits.'

'I'm sure you tipped the scales,' Milly insisted. 'Such a sense of timing. I can never thank you enough. I seem to be piling up the things I owe you. Which reminds me, I haven't given you and Keel the paintings I promised you, for saving the island. I brought them along with me, so have them now.'

The artist delved into her capacious handbag, and brought out two neatly taped boxes, both small, and both of the same shape and size. She and Keel must each have chosen miniatures, Ros saw.

Eagerly Milly held out her offerings towards them, but just as they were about to take them she seemed to hesitate, as if undecided about something, and then she swiftly crossed her hands, and offered them the opposite box instead.

'Open them,' she cried. 'I must know if you like your paintings.'

Ros cringed. What misguided impulse had caused her to ask for the painting in the first place? She could not open it, especially in front of Keel. But if she refused to look at it, Milly would want to know why, and the explanation would be even more embarrassing.

Perhaps, if she just had a peep, and then put the lid of the box down again straight away, it would satisfy

Milly. Fumbling, she prised up the lid.

A tiny circle of pale cotton wool covered the face of the miniature, and for a second that seemed to go on for hours Ros hung back. Then, at Milly's urgent, 'Well?' she drew a long breath and pushed the cotton wool aside, to reveal the painted face staring up at her from a delicate gilt frame.

The face was her own.

Shock jolted Ros. She had not asked for a portrait of herself. Milly had made a mistake. Her eyes travelled to the artist, and then, as if drawn by some irresistible magnetism, they veered to Keel, and found his look fixed on her with a peculiar intensity that increased her bewilderment.

His own box was open in his hand, and his eyes held a burning kind of excitement, as if the contents had lighted a fire in their tawny depths. To have such an effect upon him, his portrait must be of Una, Ros surmised.

Milly darted them each a puzzled look, clearly taken aback by their lack of response, and she leaned forward and peeped into Ros's box.

'Oh dear, how silly of me,' she exclaimed. 'I've given you the wrong boxes after all. You'll have to swap them over.' She turned to Walsh. 'Come and get me some supper, there's a dear. I'm starving.'

Starving? Milly, who never bothered about meals? Ros stared, but the artist was already steering the Canadian purposefully away towards the buffet tables, and Ros and Keel were left alone, marooned in a sudden sea of silence.

It went on and on. Ros's mind was in a whirl. What

did Milly mean, they would have to swap boxes? She did not want a portrait of Una. And Keel would most definitely not want a portrait of herself.

She started as he reached out a hand, and took her by the arm, and commanded, 'Come with me.'

This had all happened before. Ros felt weirdly as if she was in some kind of time warp, and each scene was being re-enacted. She jinked away from him, just as she had done at their first meeting at the airport.

'No. I . . . Milly . . .'

'Milly is a devious, scheming woman. I want to talk to you, and I can't do that in the middle of this scrum, so *come on.*'

'I don't want to talk. We've got nothing to talk about.'

His tight grip of her arm said otherwise. Keel half dragged, half guided Ros through the crowded hall, his grim-visaged look parting a path for them and making people stare after them, but he ignored them and hurried Ros out into the quiet garden at the rear of the gallery, deserted now in the softly approaching dusk.

He jerked to a halt beneath a rose arch, whose sweetly scented burden sheltered them from the sight of anyone who might happen to glance through the gallery windows, and there he spun Ros round to face him. With one hand he circled her waist, effectively preventing her escape, and he put the fingers of the other under her chin, and tipped up her face to meet his.

'Tell me what painting you asked Milly for,' he demanded.

'I—I don't remember.'

Wild horses would not drag from her the secret of her request to Milly, most especially to Keel.

'You remember perfectly well. Tell me.'

His expression was remorseless, as were his fingers cupping her chin.

'Let me go. You're hurting me.'

Keel's fingers were not hurting her nearly so much as her own, which gripped the box Milly had given to her so tightly that the sharp edge left a deep weal in the palm of her hand.

'I'll let you go after you've told me.'

His voice was harsh and brooked no refusal, but her tongue refused to form the words. She would die with humiliation if Keel learned what it was she had asked of Milly. Ros's hand gripped her box even tighter, and the increased pain in her palm gave her an idea. Mutely, she raised the miniature to show it to Keel.

His eyes glittered. 'That isn't the one. Milly said she'd made a mistake.'

'It is. It must be. She didn't.' Her voice rose, becoming incoherent, and Keel's hands shifted swiftly to her shoulders, and gave her a sharp shake.

'Ros, tell me. *I must know.*'

'No. Never.' The words were almost a sob.

'Then do as Milly said, and swap boxes.'

Swiftly Keel reached down and took Ros's box from her fingers, and pressed his own in its place.

'Look at it,' he commanded, and reluctantly she lowered her eyes to the contents.

Milly had not made a mistake after all. Her colour ebbed and flowed, and she dared not raise her eyes from the tiny painting to look at Keel. His likeness, not

Una's, looked back at her. She had got the painting she had asked for.

Which must mean . . .

The meaning exploded in her mind like a lightning bolt. The shock of it jerked her eyes upwards from the portrait in her hand to the reality standing in front of her.

'*You* . . . asked for . . . a portrait of *me*?' she whispered. 'Why?'

'You asked for a portrait of me,' Keel mocked. 'Why?'

When she did not answer he went on harshly, 'You asked for my picture because you love me. There could be no other reason. You may not know it yet. You may not want to admit it . . .'

The knowledge was beginning to spread through Ros like a forest fire, transmitted by Keel's lips as he took her mouth by storm. Frantically she fought against him, against the holocaust that was consuming her, but he held her tightly, and the fire ran unchecked through her veins, burning up her will.

She tried to cry out, but his lips covered her mouth, stifling all sound except for a tiny moan, and forcing her to come to terms with the impulse that had prompted her to ask Milly for the miniature. Not, as she had excused herself then, as a souvenir of the trip to the caves, a desire born of witchery of the music, but a deep, abiding need to have something of Keel to take away with her when she left the island.

When she left him with Una.

The image of the dark-haired girl stiffened Ros's resistance, and she began to struggle in Keel's arms. With a frantic twist of her head she wrenched her lips free, and croaked, 'Una . . .'

'What's Una got to do with us? *I love you,* Ros.'

His words stilled her as his arms could not. Ros raised incredulous eyes to his face, and he went on more softly,

'I've loved you ever since the first moment I caught sight of you, in Paris. You turned your back on me then, and you've been doing it ever since. Give me a chance, Ros. Please . . .'

Keel's voice was hoarse, begging her. Ros stared up at him as if she was seeing him for the first time.

'I thought you . . . and Una . . .' Ros got no further.

'I pandered to Una because Milly wanted me to.' The harshness was back again, unmistakable in its condemnation. 'I thought it was wrong then, and I still do, and events have proved me right.'

Events had a habit of doing just that, but Ros let it pass, and Keel went on.

'Una's gone back to her husband, and not before time. I wanted Milly to send her back long ago, but she's too soft-hearted. She was afraid Una might do something drastic if she sent her away. She couldn't see that Una was too selfish to harm herself. Events came to a head when she deliberately crashed into your sailboard, and when she set fire to the island even Milly had to come round to my way of thinking.'

He stroked the golden waves of her hair with tender fingers.

'The fire scorched your hair. I would never have forgiven Una if it had touched your lovely face as well.'

'And if it had?'

The words hurt, but Ros suddenly had to know.

'I would still have loved you, still have wanted you. Nothing will ever change that.' His eyes devoured her face, their ardent fire a promise that embraced her now and for all the years to come, as he went on, 'The upshot of it all was that Milly contacted Una's husband, and he came post haste. He still loves her, the poor fool, and he's prepared to give her a second chance.'

'I thought you loved her, too.'

'How could I, when I loved you? She doesn't even begin to compare. But you didn't want me. I longed to give you the world, and you wouldn't even accept a dress and a shawl from me.'

The anger and the anguish of her rejection roughened his voice to a growl, and Ros hesitated, but only for a moment.

'I kept your carnation,' she whispered, suddenly shy.

Keel's eyes fired. 'You kept it. Why?'

'You've just told me.'

'Tell me yourself.'

Ros searched his face. That dear, familiar face that, but for a miracle named Milly, might never have been hers except in a miniature frame.

'I love you,' she breathed.

The words were not so difficult to say, after all. They came through her softly parted lips like a sigh, but Keel caught them, and captured them with two arms straining her to him.

'Say that again,' he commanded.

'I love you . . . I love you . . .' Now it was out, she could not stop.

It was as if all the unsuspected love of those last

dreadful months burst forth like a mighty flood carrying them both on a tidal wave of Keel's kisses that covered her eyes, her cheeks, her hair, but left her mouth free to murmur the precious words over and over again, repeating his own that came haltingly, like an echo.

At last, Ros's mouth grew hungry for its share of kisses, and she reached up tender hands to his face to guide his lips back to where they belonged. Quick anguish stabbed her as she felt his cheeks wet under her fingers, the strong unmanned by tender words he had never expected to hear from her, teaching her her own strength.

An aeon passed, while time stood still, and when at last Ros leaned back in his arms, her cheeks rosy and her eyes bright, Keel confessed remorsefully, 'I was a beast to you. I made you dress my arm, and you hated it. But it was the only way I could keep you near me, get you to touch me. And that night on the terrace, I was mad with jealousy when you sang. I thought you were singing for someone else.'

'My heart must have known I was singing for you.' How clear it all seemed now. 'How blind I was.'

'We were both blind. And I was a coward. I didn't dare tell you I loved you, in case you rejected me out of hand. I had to keep some hope alive that you might one day change your mind. It took Milly to push us. She gave us the wrong boxes on purpose.'

'I wonder how she knew?'

'Fellow feeling, I expect. Milly's in love herself, with Walsh. They plan to get married after the exhibition's over.'

'But that's wonderful. I must think of a present for them.' Ros wrinkled her brow. What did an out-of-work secretary give to a wealthy woman who could buy anything she wanted?

'You've already given Milly the best present possible, by helping to make her portrait a success.' Sensitive to her every thought, Keel saw her dilemma and resolved it. 'You're staying on for the wedding,' he told her possessively, and for once his command was music to Ros's ears. 'Let's surprise them, and swap invitations?' His lips nuzzled the rising tide of colour in her cheeks. 'Marry me soon, Ros,' he whispered. 'It's been agony waiting, all these months. Don't keep me waiting any longer,' he pleaded.

'Only for as long as it takes to break the news to our families.'

'Mine won't be surprised. My letters to them have had you on every line.'

'I'm glad Milly's got Walsh to look after her.' Ros snuggled deep into his arms contentedly. 'She's so unworldly; she needs someone strong.'

'Not half so much as I need you.'

No bliss could compare to being needed by Keel. Ros twined her fingers in the drake's tail at the nape of his neck, and felt the hair curl round them like an anchor, holding her tight.

'We'll find a home in England. A real home, not a hotel. I've already got the first piece of furniture for it,' he teased, and answered Ros's round-eyed curiosity with, 'I bought Milly's painting of the windmill and the wild flowers that you liked so much. I bought it at the exhibition, and kept it, hoping against hope. But you'll have to leave it at home when you travel abroad with me.' His face suddenly sobered. 'I can't bear to part with you even for a minute. You won't be bored?' he asked her anxiously, betraying how deep was his hurt at her gibe.

'Bored? No, never with you. That was only Una and her set.'

'Oh, them.' Keel dismissed them with a wave of his hand. 'If only you had known how much I longed to buy you a wedding dress the day we went to town to buy your other clothes. There were some wonderful white dresses in the store.'

'I can wear white for my wedding.'

How glad she was that she had not given in to Lomas. That she could offer herself to the man she loved with a heart as clear as her candid gaze.

Keel stared down into her face for a long minute while the meaning of her words penetrated, then his eyes glowed, and he clasped her close in his arms and promised huskily, 'I'll give you some pearls to wear with your wedding dress. Real ones.'

'I'd rather have some pearls from the island, where I found my happiness.' Ros smiled up at him, teasing. 'You don't have to pay the earth to get something beautiful.'

'No,' Keel agreed gravely, and his eyes devoured the delicate beauty of her face. 'A marriage licence doesn't cost much.'

'Wretch!'

He laughed, and reaching out he plucked a rose from the arbour, and tucked it in her hair. 'You should always wear a flower in your hair.'

'Buy a flower for the lady,' Ros intoned.

'For luck,' Keel finished softly, and his eyes smiled. 'It worked, just as I hoped it would.'

From somewhere in the gallery, the notes of a violin floated softly through the gathering dusk, dropping through the perfumed air like tiny messengers of happiness.

'Play, gypsy,' they invited. 'Teach me to smile . . .'

From deep in the safety of Keel's arms, Ros listened, and found it easy to smile for him.

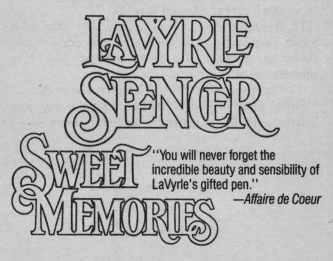
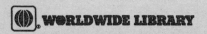

ATTRACTIVE, SPACE SAVING BOOK RACK

Display your most prized novels on this handsome and sturdy book rack. The hand-rubbed walnut finish will blend into your library decor with quiet elegance, providing a practical organizer for your favorite hard-or soft-covered books.

Only $9.95

Approximately 16" x 8" when assembled

Assembles in seconds!

To order, rush your name, address and zip code, along with a check or money order for $10.70* ($9.95 plus 75¢ postage and handling) payable to *Harlequin Reader Service:*

Harlequin Reader Service
Book Rack Offer
901 Fuhrmann Blvd.
P.O. Box 1396
Buffalo, NY 14269-1396

Offer not available in Canada.

*New York and Iowa residents add appropriate sales tax.

BKR-1A

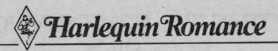

Harlequin Romance

Coming Next Month

Available in July wherever paperback books are sold, or
through Harlequin Reader Service:

In the U.S.
901 Fuhrmann Blvd.
P.O. Box 1397
Buffalo, N.Y. 14240-1397

In Canada
P.O. Box 603
Fort Erie, Ontario
L2A 5X3

Penny Jordan

Stronger than Yearning

He was the man of her dreams!

The same dark hair, the same mocking eyes; it was as if the Regency rake of the portrait, the seducer of Jenna's dream, had come to life. Jenna, believing the last of the Deverils dead, was determined to buy the great old Yorkshire Hall—to claim it for her daughter, Lucy, and put to rest some of the painful memories of Lucy's birth. She had no way of knowing that a direct descendant of the black sheep Deveril even existed—or that James Allingham and his own powerful yearnings would disrupt her plan entirely.

Penny Jordan's first Harlequin Signature Edition *Love's Choices* was an outstanding success. Penny Jordan has written more than 40 best-selling titles—more than 4 million copies sold.

Now, be sure to buy her latest bestseller, *Stronger Than Yearning*. Available wherever paperbacks are sold—in June.

STRONG-1R